H

Sermons Preached during Lent, 1864 in Great St. Mary's Church, Cambridge

SALZWASSER VERLAG

H. P. Liddon

Sermons Preached during Lent, 1864 in Great St. Mary's Church, Cambridge

Reprint of the original, first published in 1864.

1st Edition 2022 | ISBN: 978-3-75259-480-5

Verlag (Publisher): Salzwasser Verlag GmbH, Zeilweg 44, 60439 Frankfurt, Deutschland
Vertretungsberechtigt (Authorized to represent): E. Roepke, Zeilweg 44, 60439 Frankfurt, Deutschland
Druck (Print): Books on Demand GmbH, In de Tarpen 42, 22848 Norderstedt, Deutschland

SERMONS

PREACHED DURING LENT, 1864.

SERMONS

PREACHED DURING LENT, 1864

IN

Great St. Mary's Church, Cambridge.

Cambridge and London.

1864.

PREFACE.

THE Sermons contained in the present volume, and published by the kind permission of the authors, were preached at Great St Mary's Church, on the Wednesdays and Fridays during Lent, 1864. Very many of those who heard them expressed a wish that they might appear in a permanent form; and an additional reason for their publication seemed to exist, in their being a sort of first fruits of the restoration of the church, now at length actually carried out after so many difficulties and delays. The church was closed for service on the Wednesday after Easter, 1863, and was re-opened on the Purification, 1864, so that the present course of sermons followed almost immediately on its re-opening.

I can only express a hope that many who were not present while they were delivered, may derive as much advantage from reading them as those who heard them, and that in these days of danger and strife, the voice of truth may be considered to have gone forth with no uncertain sound from that church, where, in past times, so many of the greatest theologians our country has produced have delivered their testimony, and which is once more not utterly unworthy of being the church of the University and the principal church of the town of Cambridge.

H. R. L.

4, ST PETER'S TERRACE,
CAMBRIDGE.
Ascension Day, 1864.

CONTENTS.

SERMON I.

BY THE RIGHT REV. THE LORD BISHOP OF OXFORD.

GOD IN HIS PERFECTIONS THE MEASURE OF THE SINFULNESS OF SIN IN THE CREATURE.

JOB XLII. 5, 6.

PAGE

I have heard of Thee by the hearing of the ear: but now mine eye seeth Thee. Wherefore I abhor myself, and repent in dust and ashes 3

SERMON II.

BY THE REV. H. P. LIDDON.

ADAM HIDING HIMSELF FROM THE PRESENCE OF THE LORD.

GENESIS III. 8.

PAGE

And they heard the voice of the Lord God walking in the garden in the cool of the day: and Adam and his wife hid themselves from the presence of the Lord God amongst the trees of the garden 23

SERMON III.

BY THE REV. T. L. CLAUGHTON.

GOD IN HIS REVEALED PERFECTIONS THE OBJECT OF WORSHIP.

PSALM CXXX. 4.

There is forgiveness with Thee, that Thou mayest be feared . . . 53

SERMON IV.

BY THE REV. J. R. WOODFORD.

ABRAHAM STANDING BEFORE THE LORD.

GENESIS XVIII. 22.

But Abraham stood yet before the Lord 73

SERMON V.

BY THE REV. DR GOULBURN.

GOD FASHIONING THE HEARTS OF HIS PEOPLE.

ROM. VIII. 29.

PAGE

Whom He did foreknow, He also did predestinate to be conformed to the image of His Son, that He might be the firstborn among many brethren 91

SERMON VI.

BY THE REV. J. W. BURGON.

JACOB IN LIFE AND IN DEATH.

PSALM XLVI. 4.

Blessed is he that hath the GOD of Jacob for his help! . . . 115

SERMON VII.

BY THE REV. T. T. CARTER.

GOD THE HOPE AND JOY OF THE PENITENT.

S. LUKE VII. 48—50.

And He said unto her, Thy sins are forgiven. And they that sat at meat with Him began to say within themselves, Who is this that forgiveth sins also? And He said unto the woman, Thy faith hath saved thee; go in peace 141

SERMON VIII.

BY THE REV. DR PUSEY.

DAVID IN HIS SIN AND HIS PENITENCE.

PSALM LI. 4.

PAGE
Against Thee, Thee only, have I sinned 163

SERMON IX.

BY THE VERY REV. DEAN HOOK.

GOD THE CONSOLATION OF THE AFFLICTED.

LAMENTATIONS III. 32, 33.

Though He cause grief, yet will He have compassion according to the multitude of His mercies. For He doth not afflict willingly nor grieve the children of men 191

SERMON X.

BY THE REV. W. J. BUTLER.

GOD THE REWARD OF THE FAITHFUL.

PSALM XVI. 12.

Thou shalt shew me the path of life: in Thy presence is the fulness of joy: and at Thy right hand there is pleasure for evermore 225

SERMON XI.

BY THE VERY REV. DEAN GOODWIN.

MOSES WITH GOD IN MOUNT PISGAH.

DEUTERONOMY XXXIV. part of ver. 6.

PAGE
No man knoweth of his sepulchre unto this day 253

SERMON I.

GOD IN HIS PERFECTIONS THE MEASURE OF THE SINFULNESS OF SIN IN THE CREATURE.

BY

THE RIGHT REVEREND

THE LORD BISHOP OF OXFORD.

SERMON I.

JOB XLII. 5, 6.

I have heard of Thee by the hearing of the ear: but now mine eye seeth Thee. Wherefore I abhor myself, and repent in dust and ashes.

YOU will, I think, my brethren, understand the principle of selection which has set before you this night the one true measure of our sins. The whole aim of these sermons is to bring out, on successive nights, the thought of God in His various relations to us: and such a course might at any time of the year most naturally begin by shewing us, that the perfection of the adorable nature of God is in truth the measure of our sinfulness. But especially does such a subject befit the opening of Lent. For the special object of all our Lenten observance is to bring our sins before us, that our repentance for them may be deepened, and our struggle with them made more real and intense.

Now the very first condition of such a deepened penitence is that we should have some clearer insight into what sin is, in its essence. For this insight into its character is altogether needful for a due abhorrence of it. This then is why we seek for the true measure of sin:—that we may rest in no idea of it which by diminishing its evil in our eyes should make us endure its presence within us. Such a measure, then, I desire to shew you we can find only in the infinite perfections of the Lord our God.

And, first, I would pray you to observe that without some knowledge of the true God, man has no sense whatever of the evil of sin. We may at the first moment be startled by such a statement. For the very idea of sin, as sin, is one of that great range of spiritual verities with which the teaching of the Church has made all of us Christians so familiar, that we are apt to forget that our knowledge of it is derived wholly from revelation. And yet so indeed it is. And so I think we shall see it to be, if we look to those who are without such a revelation. Its working indeed has been ever active in every one of the fallen race. Its universal presence is one part of its mysterious horror. For where is it not? In our thoughts, in our desires, in the first moving of our will, in the acting of our instincts and affections, in our very prayers,—everywhere it is; pervading us as the hidden electric current pervades the extended wire—always with us. And yet man of himself has never read the solution of the terrible enigma which works with such an inward force, and with so manifold a power throughout his being. Accordingly this idea is, and ever has been, unknown to pagans and heathen. The subtle Greek philosophy, which dealt so largely and so curiously with all that concerned man; and the patient labours of the Roman moralists, were equally at fault here. There is no trace of the idea of sin, as sin, to be found amongst them all. They dealt abundantly with excesses and defects, with virtues and with vices, as affecting man's inward condition; and they could largely appreciate the evil of crime as an injury to others both singly and as a society; but there, as by an impassable barrier, their way was stopped.

To know the true meaning of the disease with much of the acting of which they were familiar, they must know its root. And to know this, they must know the character of God and the relation of man to Him. No system which did not fully recognise the perfect holiness of God and the fall of man ever did, or, so far as we can see, ever could, explain the mystery. For its essence lies in the union of these two: without a knowledge of the fall, man could not know that sin was no true part of his real being: was a stain upon it: a corruption of it: that it was not his Maker's work in him, that it was an alien usurpation under which he had been mysteriously brought, and which warred perpetually against his own truest nature. So that without revelation man looking inward on himself never could appreciate the essential evil of sin. Nor again, without the knowledge of God's holiness could there be any true standard of unholiness. With a heaven over him peopled, through the playing of his imagination upon the faint remaining vestiges of primæval tradition, with gods many and lords many, who were nothing more than the embodiment of the prolonged lines of his own various and disordered faculties, and desires, and powers, a standard of holiness was impossible to him. For where there was no knowledge of the One Holy God, there could be no knowledge of the law of God; and where there was no knowledge of law, there could be no defined sense of transgression. The inarticulate mutterings of fear, which the existence within him of an evil which he understood not, woke up in the heart of man, when the overshadowing of the supernatural spake darkly to his spirit the presence of the unknown

God, was a wholly different thing. For this, instead of revealing to him the secret of his own corruption, only affrighted him with the vision of an irresistible and malevolent power—whom he must appease often by monstrous sacrifices; by giving "the fruit of his body for the sin of his soul." But it could convey to him no true idea of the inward guilt of sin. Paganism, that is to say, had no measure of sin, because it had no certain knowledge of God in His perfections.

Next observe, that the record of God's revealing Himself to man, declares everywhere the same truth.

The patriarchal revelation, shewing little more than God's power and fatherhood, stirred up ordinarily but little sense of sin in those to whom it was made. Yet even under it, when God came indeed very nigh to His creatures, some sense of sin stirred within him as it did in Jacob when he cried out at Bethel, "Surely the Lord is in this place, and I knew it not... How dreadful is this place[1]!" More remarkably still was this consciousness of sin called forth by God's more wonderful revelation of Himself to Job. In the agony of his heart he hears suddenly the Lord answering him out of the whirlwind, and at once

[1] Gen. xxviii. 16, 17.

the vision of God wakes up in him, almost as if he were beneath the Cross of Calvary, the deep sense of an intense defilement, "Behold I am vile, what shall I answer Thee? I will lay mine hand upon my mouth[1]." "I have heard of Thee by the hearing of the ear: but now mine eye seeth Thee. Wherefore I abhor myself, and repent in dust and ashes."

The dispensation of the law followed, declaring in words, and shadowing out in all its rites and ceremonies, the holiness of God. Even in the stubborn generation to which it was given we can trace something of the fruit of this new revelation of Jehovah, in a new knowledge of the evil of sin. And as this dispensation under the power of the Spirit passed into that of the prophets, this feature meets us with a startling prominence. David under the sight of God loses all thought of the mere effects of his sin on others, terrible as in his case they had been, and pours forth all the bitterness of his soul in that one cry which marks how his high measure of the evil thing that he had done was gathered altogether from his sense of the holiness of God. "Against Thee, Thee only, have I sinned, and done this evil in Thy sight[2]." Isaiah's vision of God draws from him a like cry, "Woe is me! for I am undone; because I am a man of unclean

[1] Job xl. 4. [2] Ps. li. 4.

lips, and I dwell in the midst of a people of unclean lips: for mine eyes have seen the King, the Lord of Hosts[1]."

Thus then paganism, in its ignorance of sin, as the consequence of its ignorance of God, witnesses to us that He alone is to His creature the measure of its defilement; whilst the effects of His revelations of Himself to the Patriarchs, and under the Law and the Prophets, repeat and expand the same truth. The full light of the Church of the redeemed completes the lesson. Let us for our own practical teaching strive to follow it out. To us God has revealed, so far as man can receive them, the marvels of His incomprehensible greatness and the mystery of His Being. We know that in the essential unity of the undivided Godhead there are and ever were three co-eternal Persons—the Father, the Son, and the Holy Ghost, one God, blessed for ever. We know that the Lord our God is not merely loving, good, true, holy and just, as we see these qualities in our composite being, but that He is Love, is Goodness, is Truth, is Holiness, is Justice: that there is in Him no balance of various qualities, each checking and modifying the other, but that He is altogether and essentially that of which we have, as various qualities, certain small measures.

[1] Isa. vi. 5.

As, therefore, in the man, in whom the quality of truth is peculiarly large, there is a peculiar abhorrence of untruth, in the pure man of impurity, in the loving man of hatred, what must of necessity be the estimate of our corruptions by Him in whom as in the necessary fountain-head is the essence of that Holiness, Purity, Truth and Love, the faint transcripts of which, in humanity, constitute the qualities of the highest saint? What must be His estimate of these in us, whom of His mere love He made to be, that He might bestow on us the fullest blessedness of which a created being can be capable, in imparting Himself to us? For we know that He gave us a nature capable of finding this blessedness in serving Him: that He set us nigh to Himself in order to pour into us, even as the sunbeam pours into the light-drenched cloud, the fulness of His own radiance. We know that by the self-choice of that marvellous attribute of will which from Himself He imparted to us, in order that we as free, real, reasonable beings might be capable of loving Him, we have lost this our perfectness. We know, alas! that we ourselves, each one of us, have repeatedly renewed this evil choice; choosing and doing perversely, wilfully, or with a willing carelessness, what He hates, and refusing what He loves. Thus it is that we shew before the Infinite and the Almighty. Here then, first, for us is sin measured against the glory of the Lord. It involves a loss greater than can be estimated by the actual dimensions of a created soul, for it knows no bound, short of that perpetually elevated being and augmented blessedness which the love of the Infinite destined for His creature, through the immeasurable ages of eternity, from the perpetual imparting of Himself to the work of His hands.

And then, next, sin is measured for us by God's redeeming as by His creating love. For when we were thus lost, the counsels of His unfathomable Wisdom planned our restoration through the incarnation, sacrifice, suffering, and atonement of the co-eternal Son. Here again the perfection of God is the only measure of the malignity of sin. For what it is, we may see, if anywhere, in this awful sacrifice. For though we cannot, with our poor intelligences pretend to understand all the deep necessities which required the suffering of the Son of God, yet thus much we may see, that so intense a contradiction is there in the creature's perverted will to the Will of God, that only by the Eternal Son knitting to Himself, in His own Divine Personality, that nature, and offering it up in the spotless sacrifice of Himself, could its sinfulness be atoned for; only by conveying that nature, sanctified in Himself, to us, and with it the indwelling of the Holy Ghost, could its tyranny be cast out. Look then at this tremendous sacrifice demanded by the Justice of God and provided by his Mercy and Love, and measure by it the malignity of sin. And then remember that though this one offering were sacrifice enough for the sins of the whole world, that it was needed not because there was a world of transgressors, but because there was any sin; for *one* sin required all this costly offering. Without that blood-shedding, not for *one* sin was there remission; if the first sin had ended man's course, if there had been no successive generations of evildoers, yet would all this atonement, all this healing have been needed, and that one sin must have brought Christ from Heaven, or humanity was lost. For by it the creature God had made in His image to love and glorify Him in His own perpetual blessedness, had fallen away for ever from His perfectness; and this, which is true of that first sin, is true of every separate act of wilful sin which we or any of the fallen race ever have committed. Every one needed the whole sacrifice of Christ for its forgiveness. Here then is sin's measure. And if anything could be added it were this, that in us it is a wilful choice of this malignant evil against the love of Redemption and the love of Renewal, against the cross of Christ, against the Holy Spirit's striving. And here is a new malignity in sin of which only Christians can be guilty. For they only can sin against all the mercies of the regenerate state: they only can do this despite to the Spirit of grace: they only can trample under-foot the Son of God, and count the blood of the covenant an unholy thing; they only can crucify the Lord afresh, and put Him to an open shame. So that here again the perfection of God's wisdom and love and power, which beam forth in our redemption, mark with a new intensity the sinfulness of sin. Thus then I say, brethren, is sin measured. And it is of the utmost moment that we so measure it, in order really to understand its essential malignity, and see what, unless it be cast out of the creature by the Creator's power, it must work in him. For it is in him a principle of intense rebellion in his central will, and from that centre in his every part, against the blessed perfection of the Eternal God. And what can end this? Under every process, framed by Infinite Love and Wisdom for the recovery of His creature, with all provided which His Almighty Power can give to work out His purposes of Love; with all done, save the crushing out of its will, which would indeed be the *un*making a reasonable moral agent, the creature has refused to be restored—has chosen for itself that to which the necessary Will and Being of the Holy One is an eternal contradiction. How shall change visit it more, save in the ever-increasing hatred and torment of an ever-deepening despair, as the evil within itself intensifies its malignity by perpetual action, and casts itself more and more forth through the whole life of him whom it possesses, in absolute and hating contradiction to the centre of all holiness and bliss. Here then we may see that it is only by the perfection of God that sin can be measured. For whilst the essential evil of sin is present, in all its reality, in its least acting, no creaturely being, not even the highest, can measure all its malignity, because for ever and for ever it is capable of developing into a more intense and hating rebelliousness of despair, the whole being of the lost one in whom it is perpetually working. From all which there follow some practical conclusions, which it most eminently concerns us to gather and to note.

First see what, in the light of this truth, is the real meaning and consequence of that denial which we meet with now on many sides of the awful truth, "They that have done evil shall go into everlasting fire." This denial recommends itself by urging that it is only a full declaration of the Fatherly Love of

God which would fain at last bring every reasonable creature to happiness. But mark what, in the sight we have had of the malignity of sin, it really is.

First, it is a charging upon God *all* the sufferings of fallen humanity. For if consistently with His blessed Nature He can at last so alter the will which against grace has chosen rebellion, what were it but cruelty to wait till the end of the supposed ages of suffering to effect that which, on this supposition, He must, against the creature's will, effect for him at last, and so might, if he would, accomplish at the first. The whole Gospel scheme repeats to us that there is some deep necessity in the kingdom of grace which leaves it to the will of each man to yield to or to resist the drawings of God's grace. Why this is so we cannot tell. It may be that hereafter, in the Kingdom, we shall gaze, as we adore their majesty, into the depth of these hidden counsels of His love, though here we can but bow submissively to that which He has told us, and though He willeth not the death of a sinner, but rather that he should turn from his sin and be saved, He has said, "The soul that sinneth it shall die." But this teaching unsays the awful sentence; proclaims that there is no necessity in God's nature for the sinner's death, but that whensoever it pleases Him, He can, consistently with His own holiness, so act upon the sinner as to free him from his sin. And in so doing, this miserable theory charges upon the God of love every anguish which in any one of His creatures is thus needlessly permitted to intervene before the accomplishment of His final work of restoration.

Secondly. This denial does really rob every man of hope in the Personal God, and leads him into those dreary mists of Pantheism which border hard upon the thick darkness which settles down upon the Atheist. For as we have seen, the evil malignity of sin is a necessary correlative of the existence and perfections of the Personal God, of which it is the wilful contradiction in the creatures. Any theory therefore which denies the malignity of sin denies, by necessary consequence, the perfections of the ever-blessed God. He then who teaches that sin instead of being this eternal contradiction of God, is something which one day God will, by a mere act of power, remove from His creature, and that its endless punishment would be a merciless and so an intolerable cruelty, does really, however unintentionally, subvert the foundation of all real belief in God. By degrees with such an one all earnest faith perishes. From him, erring thus deeply, there fades away first the Atonement, and then the reality of Grace, then the certainty of Revelation, then the mystery of the Eternal Trinity, then the very personality of God, and then His Presence with us, His hearing our prayers, His fashioning our hearts; until the bewildered man is left in the thick fog bred of his own self-will; without the lights of heaven above, without the landmarks of the Church around Him; sin and salvation, the present and the future, the eternal reward and the endless punishment, all equally obscured; and with these, the sight of the countenance of the reconciled Father bent over him in love, the pierced hand of the Eternal Son leading him into the Presence, and the perpetual moulding of the blessed and eternal Spirit through sacraments and means of grace, all equally lost, and lost too often for ever, to the doubting, shivering, disturbed soul.

But note a third consequence, and that most deeply concerning every one of us, of the conclusions we have reached as to the malignity of sin when measured by the perfections and holiness of God. That deadly evil is in every one of us. It is in us in our fallen nature. It is struggling, it may be ruling in us. All the malignity of this rebellion against God is in every wilful sin we commit, or ever have committed. Nay, without great and alarming acts of sin which might startle our conscience, and lead us to repentance, the whole habit of our souls may be a perpetual choosing of our own will, and our own way, and so one perpetual resistance to the Will of God. To overcome this rebellion is one special object of our life. What are we doing, what have we ever done, for its accomplishment? Are we seeking for deliverance? Are we indeed watching, praying, struggling, fighting hard against the evil we are set to overcome? Or, are we allowing it in ourselves, and encouraging it in others? Are we calling it by fair names, covering it with soft excuses, dealing with the inward plague as if it were harmless, allowable or inevitable? What answer to such questions do our hours of prayer, our Chapel attendances, our Communions, our amusements, our social gatherings, our tone of conversation, our use of time, make? Is this unspeakable contradiction of the blessed nature of our God hardening in us? Are lust, or excess, or idleness, or indulged self-will strengthening and perfecting it? Let us closely search into ourselves and dare to meet the answer which our consciences deliver. Only let us be in earnest in the search. Not massing lazily our sins together, and resting fatally content in a mere general estimate of our condition, taken with all the blind flattering partiality of our own self-love, but striving earnestly to weigh the guilt of every separate act of rebellious self-will, which has made strong within us the power of evil. O beloved brethren, redeemed of Christ, striven with by the Spirit, cared for by the Father's love, cast not away your inestimable birthright. Young men, foster not within your yet plastic natures this deadly sickness. Old men, ye have but an hour to live. Oh! seize upon this remaining moment to find deliverance from this endless ruin. Resolve in God's strength this very Lent, this very night, to cast out the evil one. Resolve, and then begin to act, to act in earnest in little daily things, and the victory is sure.

Pray in earnest. Read daily some verses of your Bibles. Take some time, daily if possible, weekly at least, for self-searching, and for meditation. Break through some evil habit. Get rid of the law of idle self-pleasing: of the indolent rebellion of sloth, or the active rebellion of self-will in life or in religion. Yea, recast your life if need be, on the pattern of the Son of Man. Cry mightily to the loving healer against the soul-sickness which is in you. Only be in earnest in crying to Him. The cold, languid, formal prayer of the half-hearted, has no wings with which to mount up to Him. This coldness is the very chill of death; but cry in earnest, and thou shalt be heard. Call upon Him in those words of agonizing supplication, "O Son of David, have mercy on me—Thou that takest away the sin of the world, have mercy on me." Cry and wait, and watch and strive, and all shall yet be well. The presence of the personal God, as thou hast never known it, shall be round about thee. Angel hands shall quicken thy tarrying flight. The infinite powers of the blessed Spirit shall work within thee; the face of Him who died to redeem thee, thorn-crowned as He was to save thee, shall be bent upon thee; and thou, too, by the measure of His Love shalt learn the measure of thy sin, and shalt be taught to give thyself with all thou hast and art to Him who gave Himself for thy redemption.

SERMON II.

ADAM HIDING HIMSELF FROM THE PRESENCE OF THE LORD.

BY

THE REV. H. P. LIDDON, M.A.

STUDENT OF CHRIST CHURCH, AND EXAMINING CHAPLAIN TO THE LORD BISHOP OF SALISBURY.

SERMON II.

GENESIS III. 8.

And they heard the voice of the Lord God walking in the garden in the cool of the day: and Adam and his wife hid themselves from the presence of the Lord God amongst the trees of the garden.

THERE are many considerations amply sufficient to prove to thoughtful Christians that the earliest chapters of the Book of Genesis, as all the other chapters in the Bible, are strictly, historically, as a whole and in detail, true. Some of those considerations can only be accurately estimated by scholars; but we all of us can do justice to one particular line of thought, which helps us to hold fast such a belief, and which it is my object to bring before you this evening.

It may have chanced to some of us to have lighted unexpectedly upon an old family portrait. Before us is a likeness of an ancestor, from whom we are directly descended, and whose day of life was parted from our own by an interval of two or three hundred years. We are at first arrested by the points of contrast between this relic of the past, and our present life. The very frame which holds the painting speaks of another age. The whole setting and colouring of the work is strange to us. The dress, the hair, the formal posture, each contribute to increase our sense of distance from the subject of the picture. The hands certainly are like our own hands, yet they are folded or displayed in a way which would be unnatural to us. The lines of the countenance have a marked fixedness, a rigidity; and perhaps we involuntarily bethink ourselves of some narrow sphere of thought, or contracted sympathies, which must have cramped the brain or heart of our progenitor. Yet, underlying all these differences, penetrating them, first drawing our attention only partially away from them, and so distracting us, and then finally absorbing it altogether, and throwing the points of difference, fairly and thoroughly into the shade, there is a something which rivets us, which connects us with the portrait, by the fascination of an internal sympathy. At first we cannot plainly say what it is; we are drawn on by a vague undefinable impression. Gradually we analyze that impression; we discover a certain determinate point or points of resemblance; there is an expression in the eye, or a curve of the lip, or a line across the brow, which cannot be mistaken; it is THE characteristic of our family; more or less distinctly it is repeated in all our living relations, here strongly and obviously, there faintly and scarcely with sufficient distinctness to be traced by a stranger;—but when once we have recognized the correspondence between the quaint portrait of another age and the living type of our own, we do not need to turn the picture, that we may see if it has a name and date at the back; we say at once—"That is one of my ancestors."

Now, something like this is the experience of the great human family, when it looks at that portrait of Adam, the falling and fallen Adam, at the beginning of Genesis. All the setting of that portrait is as far removed from the present as possible. Indeed we can only realize the greatness of the interval by counting up the successive intervening stages. How unlike is human life now to human life in the middle ages! What a difference again between the middle ages and the period of the Incarnation! Or between the date of our Lord's Birth and the age of David or Moses! or, again, between Moses and the early Patriarchs, whether Abraham or Noah! Or, finally, between Noah and our first parent, when man had not yet made himself at home in the world, and was at the very fountain-head of his history. Indeed, between this primal time and our modern civilization there is so sharp and startling a contrast, that to certain minds, weak of faith, and given to the culture of fancy-theories, the history of Adam reads as if it were merely a higher kind of poetry, with which the rich imagination of a later age had endeavoured to fill up and to decorate the presumed blank of man's earliest history. Any such hypothesis is, of course, hopelessly at issue with a true belief in Holy Scripture as the infallible Word of God, guaranteed by His Wisdom and His Truth. But the existence of such an error is here noted as illustrating the extraordinary distance which is felt to sever us, the men of to-day, from the outward manner of life of our First Parent.

Yet that distance contracts sensibly beneath our gaze till at length it seems to vanish outright, when we turn the soul's eye upon the moral likeness, or rather the moral unity which links us, the children of the 19th century, to our first natural Parent. If the story of the Fall had been merely shaped or invented by a human poet out of the human traditions around him, or out of the resources of his own heart or head, his Adam would have been idealized. A sentiment of irrepressible reverence for the first of men, would have veiled in our father the weakness of common humanity, and would have anticipated by forty centuries all that poor human nature could anticipate, of the image of a Sinless and Impeccable Christ.

Narrowing down our thoughts, then, this evening to one cardinal point of likeness between Adam and ourselves, let us endeavour to estimate and draw some useful lessons from that instinct of self-concealment which shows itself in our first Parent as an immediate and almost involuntary consequence of his sin. "They heard the voice of the Lord God walking in the garden in the cool of the day: and Adam and his wife hid themselves amongst the trees of the garden."

I. Now that which strikes us first of all, is, that Adam represents the average sinner. A man may do worse than Adam. Many men have done and do worse than hide themselves from God after outraging Him by sin. Adam's conduct proves that the sense of God's Presence, Awfulness, Greatness, was still intact in his soul. There are sins which burn out and destroy that sense. There are men who sin, and then look their Creator in the face and bid Him defiance. There are others who, feeling the absurdity as well as the gigantic risks of this procedure, endeavour to persuade themselves that they can bring their belief in God into harmony with their sin. For them, perchance, God is not a Being Who exists, as He is, whether they recognize Him or no, but only a 'thought,' a 'conception,' an 'idea'—in point of fact, a mere creation of their own minds. This being so, it is obvious to such persons to prune and fashion the 'idea' of God, as their lower instincts may suggest. You remember the noble passage in Isaiah's later poetry, where the Prophet pours forth the scorn of a holy soul upon the idolatries of Babylon, with which the captive people would shortly after be brought into such intimate contact. He is describing the idol-manufacturer, who worships the idol which he constructs; and who uses for domestic purposes the very material which he adores: "He burneth part thereof in the fire; with part thereof he eateth flesh; he roasteth roast, and is satisfied; yea, he warmeth himself, and saith, Aha, I am warm, I have seen the fire. And the residue thereof he maketh a god, even a graven image; he falleth down unto it, and worshippeth it, and prayeth unto it, and saith, Deliver me; for thou art my god...He feedeth on ashes, a deceived heart hath turned him aside, that he cannot deliver his soul, nor say, Is there not a lie in my right hand[1]?" Now this process thus described, is by no means confined to workers in wood and metal: it is possible to do the same thing with such material as human thought. It is only too easy to construct an idol within the "den" of our spirits, out of the mental matter which we employ for our daily and even sinful purposes. The idol is not less an idol, because it is ideal and immaterial; its incorporeal thinness is a fresh element of danger; we see no form and paint with our bodily eyes, and we are forthwith thrown off our guard. But there it is, meanwhile, throned, crowned, sacrificed to, adored within the sanctuary of the soul. There it is, this creation of our speculation, or of our "consciousness," or of our prejudices, or of our debased instincts, exacting the homage which is due only to Him Who reigns in heaven. We see this idolatry going on beneath our eyes; and the history of unfaithful Israel repeats itself in the heart of Christendom. Most of the idolatries into which the Israelites fell were subtle-forms of nature-worship; the processes of nature were personified, and the sensuous idol attracted the people, while the idea held the allegiance of the higher minds of the day. In our own time physical law is being erected into a conception which limits, or imprisons, or annihilates

[1] Is. xliv. 16, 17. 20.

and supplants God, although the full measure of the mischief may be at first imperfectly apprehended. And men justify sin, by representing sin as a necessity; it illustrates a law, and surely, man cannot be held free, when God Himself is said to be vanishing into a remote heaven at the bidding of modern thought, behind a network of laws which annihilate His Freedom. Or again, a more common modification of the Revealed Nature of God, in accordance with the debased instincts and necessities of sin, is the theory of Universalism. God, we are told, is Benevolence, but He is not Justice; or He is only Justice in such sense that ultimately His Justice, although unsatisfied, must cede to His Benevolence. He has created, as the expression of His mercy, an endless heaven, but He has not created, as the expression of His righteous hatred of sin, an endless hell. A common, yet how fatal and soul-withering a delusion! A conception of God, mark you, which differs from the God of Heaven, from the God of Holy Scripture and of the Catholic Church, no less vitally than did the calves of Dan and Bethel from the Lord Jehovah. The god of Universalism may be an intellectual and fascinating creation: but he is a creation of earth; he is not a reality in heaven; he is a modification, a mutilation of, and so a substitute for the Being Whom we know to be indeed (blessed be His Holy Name) infinitely Merciful, but also infinitely Holy, and infinitely Just. And now, as of old, "they that go after other gods shall have great trouble." It may give a momentary and delusive relief—it can never give lasting peace and rest to abandon the creed and worship of Jerusalem for the gilded intellectual idols, who are incensed, whether occasionally in the high places of Samaria, or continually in the marts of Tyre.

Now Adam, writhing with the first agonies of that fresh and ghastly wound, which sin had inflicted on his conscience, could not attempt these complicated insults against the Being of God. They are audacities proper to a later time, when faith is feeble, and sin repeated and gigantic in its efforts. Such sin has good reason for not wishing to retain God[1] in its knowledge, as He is; and its inclinations, like Balak, always will seek for prophets to give them shape, utterance, and even respectability. Adam, sinner as he was, was fresh from the purity and the Presence of Eden. He had watched his Creator too intimately and too often to doubt His essential Attributes of Power and Justice. And therefore, "when they heard the voice of the Lord God walking in the garden in

[1] Rom. i. 28.

the cool of the day, Adam and his wife hid themselves from the presence of the Lord God among the trees of the garden."

II. They "hid themselves." It was not the result of a consultation; it was an instinct. They could not justify their act by reason; but we do not reason at times of excitement, or of fear, or of agony. We act by impulse, *i. e.* in obedience to the pressure of some dominant passion or motive, which sways our whole will, and to which we involuntarily yield ourselves. Two such motives would concurrently have determined the act of Adam.

(*a*) Of these the first was *Fear*. Adam knew by intuition and by experiment the awful greatness of God. He had a consciousness of God's Power and resources, of which our enfeebled intellects can form but a scant conception. This knowledge had, up to the time of his sin, only deepened his love of God. Each new Attribute or Virtue which he discovered in his Infinite Creator, only provoked some new movement of love or adoration within his holy soul. For as yet, nothing had passed, which should rightly lead him to regard the Being, Who had given him life, beauty, strength, and thought, Who had crowned the gifts of nature with the sanctities of grace, Who had placed him, as the lord of earth, in its choicest Paradise—with other feelings than those of trustful and adoring love. But when sin had entered into the world, it was otherwise. Sin at once snapped the chain of Love which had hitherto bound man to the heart of God. But it left intact man's knowledge of what God had been to him: the knowledge of God only perishes outright when, through continuous sin, men or races of men, become, as the Apostle points out to us, utterly reprobate. In a certain terrible way, sin even added to Adam's knowledge. Before his fall Adam had indeed a knowledge of good; he had that sort of knowledge which is possible to innocence. He knew good directly; he did not know it, happily for himself, by experience of that which is contrary to it. Evil is a science in itself; and now, as in Paradise, those proud tempers who will not listen to the gospel of good, learn true but terrible lessons from the gospel of evil. They who are intimate with evil, do in one sense know more than they who only know good; but their larger knowledge need not be envied them. They pay dearly for their experience; the truth is forced on their acceptance by a "reductio ad horribile." It is surely better to trust a mother at once, than to find out that she was right after all, from the bitter consequences of neglecting the gentle warnings of her anxious love.

In some such way it was that Adam after his sin still looked at God, but looked at Him as he looked at life, from another side. The forbidden fruit had given Adam the key of the science of evil. But would Infinite Power crush that which Infinite Goodness could not but condemn? Adam indeed knew that he must die; but what was death? was it the severance of soul and body, or the ruin of both? was it stupor or was it annihilation? was it to be an agony or a relief? True! God was still there; but His greatness was now the measure of the terror of the creature who had dared to disobey Him; so "Adam hid himself from the presence of the Lord God among the trees of the garden." It was an act of fear.

(β) But it was also an act of *Shame*. Fear must have been to Adam a strange sensation, although in a distant way it was allied to the adorations of his life of sanctity. At this moment in heaven, the highest creatures fear a holy fear, while yet in truth and perfectness they love their mighty Creator. The slavish fear which perfect love casts out hath torment; but the godly fear of the blessed is an essential element of adoration. In this way Adam had felt a fear of God in his unfallen life which differed from the cowering fear of his guilty conscience, much as a healthy circulation of the blood might differ from the pulse of fever. But shame was an absolutely new thing, unlike any other capacity or experience in himself with which our first father had been previously acquainted. No sooner had he sinned than shame followed upon the act, as an effect upon its cause. It was a tide of conscious confusion which poured within over the faculties of his soul; but it was also a something which expressed itself without in the very framework of his body; it mantled visibly over his countenance and betrayed to the eye the processes of his secret life. While painfully aware of it, he could not check or control it; the effort to do so would but stimulate the mischief, since it would deepen his sense of its cause. It was a resistless impulse; he must needs hide himself; he would find relief beneath the shadow of the trees; or at least he would find relief in seeking it. Shame! a sensation, brethren, which sinners only know; which would have formed no part of the life of human feeling but for sin; which does not indeed survive repetitions of sin, since it is the fresh protest of truth and purity against the power which threatens, and which in time accomplishes their banishment from the soul. O most mysterious and singular witness for the honour of man and for the rights of God, which comes to us, as did Nathan to David, at the crisis of our humiliation, and reveals it to our unwilling vision in all its degrading significance!

And as the greatness of God was the measure of Adam's fear, so his own lost greatness was the measure of Adam's shame. We learn what he must once have been, partly from the surviving beauties of the ruined nature which he has transmitted to us his children, partly from the higher beauty of his Mighty Antitype, our Lord and Saviour. Each perfection which Adam had forfeited was a new provocative to shame. That kingly sway over nature,—that freedom of his body from suffering, and from death,—that intellectual vigour, which seems to have anticipated science, and which was crowned by revelation,—that harmony of all the faculties of the soul—that spotless innocence, that unclouded heart, that buoyant tide of hope which had a right to expect everything, and had never yet been checked—these and much more were gone. He had been a child of grace; his faculties were now dismantled and disorganized; the passions had revolted against the will; and the will had rebelled against the rule of conscience; conscience itself was no longer a true reflection of the light of heaven and of the Will of God. And then it was so easy to have obeyed. Infidels, indeed, have scoffed at God's precept to Adam, as if it had been a senseless command for which no adequate motives could be alledged, and which if irrationally and thoughtlessly violated, might yet have been violated without serious guilt. But here is a confusion of thought between a general law and a particular application. Adam, by the terms of creation, had come into existence as a being who had to love God as his proper duty. "Thou shalt love the Lord thy God with all thy heart." The law of Sinai, and the law of the Gospel, was also the law of Adam's conscience. It could not be otherwise; it is absolutely inconceivable that God could create a free and thinking being, without this intervening law of love, linking the creature in its freedom to its great Creator. But such a law must have a test, a touchstone, to be real; and the meaning of Adam's disobedience is to be read, not in the particular act of eating the fruit, but in the ascertained relation of that act to his debt of love and loyalty towards God. Some other test might possibly have been devised; something else might conceivably have been forbidden or enjoined. Yet the very simplicity of this test, which is a signal proof of God's mercy, is by rationalism turned against Him. Some test was clearly necessary; it was necessary to the greatness and freedom of Adam's service; for to have been absolutely removed from danger would be to have offered, not a moral, but a necessitated obedience to the Author of life. Yet in that simple test —"Thou shalt not eat"—Adam failed. He failed at the first suggestion and without resistance; he failed, in spite of all the ascertained blessings and joys and greatnesses of Paradise; he failed, though for an infinitely contemptible object; he failed, in spite of the threat of death, as the penalty of failure; he failed, as if for no better reason than that continued obedience was an irritating monotony;—and when he had thus failed, and the consequences of failure were pouring in as a flood upon his soul, shame must have been almost a relief, just as pain of body is at times better than sheer insensibility. Shame was at least natural; aye, we doubt not, it was very natural for Adam to cower amongst the trees of the garden.

III. "Amongst the trees of the garden." It seems to us a rude and senseless expedient. So no doubt it was; only, in that earliest age, how to hide from God had not as yet been elaborated into an accomplishment. That which Adam attempted by seeking the shadow of the trees is compassed by men of our own day by various well-known expedients. God speaks to conscience, whether to the conscience of the hardened sinner, or to the conscience of the man who is balancing between heaven and hell. We hear the voice of the Lord God walking in the garden of His Church, in the cool of the day of life. For the moment all else is hushed; passion, prejudice, worldly opinion, the pleadings of lower interests and of gross but strong habits—all are silent; and we hear That Voice. He is speaking already, but afar off; we have an indistinct sense of what He must be saying; we know that presently, He will be face to face with us, He will speak with terrible plainness. He will speak to our inmost soul; He will speak as He spoke to Levi, to the rich young man, to St Paul, to Felix. Shall we wait and listen? That is the question. "To listen," we say, "would be to increase responsibility." So we say to ourselves, forgetting that we are already responsible for that which is offered and which we reject, no less truly than for that which is refused after full consideration; although of course in the last case there is a more damning note of reprobation than in the first. But it is at this point precisely, that men take the fatal resolution, or rather, that they yield to the irrational impulse which is dictated by fear and shame,—the impulse to hide themselves.

And what are the trees beneath the shade of which the human soul seeks refuge from its God? What are the popular expedients resorted to for spiritual self-concealment? (1) Pleasure, an uninterrupted round of excitements, or even of sensual indulgences, that is one expedient, and the most obvious to coarser natures. Certainly, after a while, it palls upon us, it becomes a labour and a drudgery. But it cannot be given up; even when it is a positive anguish, it must still be clung to, as the blister which may draw out to the surface of thought some of that internal irritation which the festering wound of sin has lodged within the soul, and which craves for a Divine relief. There are moments indeed when men feel that this expedient does not really serve them; on the very eve of his ruin the Eastern king beheld from amidst his luxuries and his sensualities the stern handwriting which was traced by the finger of God upon the wall of destiny. (2) Occupation—that is another hiding-place. Bury the sensibilities of conscience beneath a vast accumulation of work. Work at any rate is duty; and conscience *may* be morbid. So we speak; and there is thus a respectability about this expedient which ensures it a certain popularity among those who, although not at peace with God, are on the best possible terms with society. They argue that man being finite, is only capable of a certain measure of energy and feeling; and they would drain this energy off in the direction of mechanical or mental labour, so that the faculties may be too entirely prostrated to listen to the Voice, or to start into healthful terror at the sight of God. And then their work does undeniably achieve a certain amount of intellectual, or social, or even of moral good; and they cherish the hope that, even if the malady within should be organic, it cannot be absolutely fatal. Even if the voice of God be plain, neglect will not be an unrelieved insult; since the outward activities of life will in reason be accepted as a sort of compensation for their neglect of the central and spiritual demands of conscience. Miserable delusion! when thought, time, resolution are spent in laying out an ornamental garden around what was once a palace, but is now a ruin,—in decking the chamber of spiritual death with the conveniences and ornaments that might have once been grateful or useful to its living occupant. All work that is not done for God, and with the sunshine of His smile upon it, is lost work, and worse than lost: and no work, however magnificent and striking be its outward and material results, can be work for God, while, at the very centre of his being, the workman shrinks from facing God, and cowers timidly beneath the thicket of a ceaseless outward occupation. (3) Once more there is moral rationalism, the desperate effort of the soul to persuade itself that sin is not what God has pronounced it to be, and that the voice of God in conscience is but a sickly and disreputable scruple, unworthy of the strong thought of an enlightened age. Men who, perhaps from a lack of intellectual enterprise, do not venture to construct for themselves a new god, will nevertheless build a hiding-place from the face of Him in Whom they still cannot but believe; they will build up in their souls the labyrinth of a false conscience. They will accept the moral teaching of the Gospel, only so far as it may be echoed by the voice of depraved nature, or accepted by the social necessities of their day. All that is sublime, heroic, severe—all that reveals the life of the creature in its true relative insignificance before the Eye of the Creator, yet in its true greatness and awfulness as well,—all that reflects the supernatural and that vindicates God to man as a living God,—all self-denial, self-discipline, penance, sustained prayer, high views of duty, the mysteries of responsibility, and the mysteries of grace—they will have none of it. Public opinion—so true and safe a guide for material concerns and for all that ends with the grave—so rotten and despicable a substitute for His voice Who Alone has revealed to man the unseen world—public opinion dictates the major premises of the false conscience. The man forthwith gets within the hut which he has constructed; he persuades himself that he is comfortable; he is not unconscientious after his measure and kind; he takes a free and easy view of life and duty; and he acts up to his self-made theory. It will do very well, my brethren, as long as it lasts; it will do, until the roof of his little manufactory of darkness is shattered by a bolt from the judgment-seat of the Lord of Light... Certainly Adam, our first parent, in the freshness of his first sin, knew nothing of these expedients of his unscrupulous descendants. And they, with the receipts which each new rationalism supplies for crushing out the sense of sin, and for hiding from the face and voice of God, may naturally smile at the simplicity, while they may even pity the extremity of their first parent—reduced in his weakness and nakedness to hide himself even "amongst the trees of the garden."

IV. It is easy for us to form an estimate of Adam's act in hiding from the Presence of God. For the moment, we imagine ourselves as lookers on; and we have little difficulty in passing judgment upon conduct for which, or for the like of which, we believe ourselves to be in no way responsible. Only the other day, in this spirit, one half of the English people formed a deliberate judgment upon the act of the Danish General de Meza in retreating from his lines of fortification: and in like manner, as believing themselves to be judging something outside them, and with which they have nothing whatever to do, the human family have no difficulty in characterizing the endeavour of their first parent to hide himself from the presence of the Lord among the trees of the garden as "foolish" and "irrational."

Yes, my brethren, it was foolish: it was irrational. But why? Because it was to attempt the impossible. This first; and next, because it was to fly from the one hope and opening for restoration and safety.

Need I say it, there is no such thing as flying from God. The Omnipotent is everywhere. In heaven, doubtless, after a manner appreciable to saints and angels, who are irradiated by His glory and who worship His perfections; but also on earth, so that, as if He were an encompassing atmosphere, each one of us "in Him lives, and moves, and has his being." All life is but the outflow of His self-existent, pervading Vitality: all that lives and is, would presently fall back into its original nothingness, were He for one moment to withdraw His sustaining Hand. Thus it comes to pass, that He is in a manner present even in the gloom of the Eternal Pit, although the lost are reft of all sense of His Presence, and their agony consists in that special deprivation, no less than in the pain of sense to which they are condemned. Most intimately is He present to the inmost vibrations of the life of all spiritual beings; nay, so intimately, that no faculty of a soul can vary its attitude ever so delicately towards the faculties beside it, without the whole moral meaning of the variation being perfectly open to His unerring gaze. It follows from the very idea of God that all things are naked and open to Him with Whom we have to do. He would not be God, if it were not certain that to Him all hearts are open, all desires known, and that from Him no secrets are hid. No Psalm places the creature with greater truth and directness beneath the searching, penetrating gaze of the Creator than the 139th:—

> O God, Thou hast searched me out, and known me.
> Thou knowest my down-sitting, and mine uprising;
> Thou understandest my thoughts long before.
> Thou art about my path, and about my bed,
> And spiest out all my ways.
> For lo! there is not a word in my tongue
> But Thou, O God, knowest it altogether.
>
> Ps. cxxxix. 1—3.

And then there presently follows a practical reflection:

> Whither shall I go then from Thy Spirit?
> Or whither shall I go from Thy presence?
> If I climb up into heaven, Thou art there;
> If I go down to hell, Thou art there also.

If I take the wings of the morning,
And remain in the uttermost part of the sea,
Even there also shall Thy Hand lead me,
And Thy Right Hand shall hold me.
If I say, Peradventure the darkness shall cover me,
Then shall my night be turned into day.
Yea, the darkness is no darkness with Thee,
But the night is as clear as the day:
The darkness and light to Thee are both alike.

Ibid. vv. 6—11.

In short, to attempt to fly from God is only to practise a trick upon oneself. We cannot achieve the impossible; but we can persuade ourselves to forget it as being such. True! this is the resource of weakly natures; but it is common enough. Just as, among the lower creatures there are some which have been observed, when at the point of becoming the prey of large beasts or serpents, to shut their eyes, that, if it were only for a moment, they might taste the luxury of forgetting their cruel and inevitable fate; so there are men who know that since God exists, God is everywhere, within as without them; yet who inconsistently think to fly from His presence; who dream of a life in some corner of creation where He is not; and who end by persuading themselves for a year or two that they have succeeded in realising it.

But also: if we *could* escape from God—how piteously unwise! If in this life He pursues us with His providences, so that we continually hear Him, moving at a little distance from us, and seeking an interview —why is it? Why does the self-existent Creator, so complete in His Blessedness and His Resources, thus track and dog the steps of the weak and sinful creatures that His Hands have made? Men nourish suspicious thoughts of God, as if He would not leave them to themselves, as if He had something to gain by seeking them. Yet they might see in a human father's love for his child a faint shadow of that Boundless Charity Which having freely given us life, and having hung upon the Cross of shame that that gift of Life might not, through our waywardness, have become our bane, pursues us through our term of days with ceaseless solicitations, urging us to meet Love by love, and to return as children to the arms of our most tender Parent. "God so loved the world, that He gave His Only-begotten Son, that whosoever believeth in Him should not perish, but have everlasting life[1]." There is the cause of acceptance: here the more ancient invitation. "Turn ye even to me with all your heart, and with fasting, and with weeping, and with mourning; and rend your heart, and not your garments, and turn unto the Lord your God: for He is gracious and merciful, slow to anger, and of great kindness, and repenteth Him of the evil[2]." Thus

[1] St John iii. 16. [2] Joel ii. 12, 13.

it is, brethren, that this very Lent your God is bidding you look Him in the Face. You Christians have less excuse than Adam for shunning God, by crouching beneath the trees, whether of pleasure, or occupation, or of false and dark theories about Him. You know the meaning, the full and blessed meaning of that Promise of Love which was made to Adam only when He had come forth from his hiding-place, about the "Seed of the woman who was to bruise the serpent's head." The Blood of the Most Holy which flowed of old in an atoning stream on Calvary, flows on through the centuries of the Church, giving power to her Sacraments, and strength and acceptance to her stream of ceaseless prayer, and certainty and effect to her pardon of sin. Jesus has lived and died; Jesus intercedes in glory; Jesus, reigning in heaven, yet present with His Church to the end of time, bridges over the chasm between earth and heaven, and makes it possible for the hardest and vilest and lowest of sinners to pass forth from his degradation and defilement into the Eternal Presence, aye, and to gaze with unfaltering eye upon the Spotless Purity of God.

One thing is needed. We must be true. Truth is at the bottom of all real excellence, whether in action or speculation, whether in the concerns of earth or in the things of heaven. Cost what it may, we must be true. We must seek to see ourselves *as we are.* We must seek to see God, after our measure, *as He is*, and with our eye fixed on Him, to show ourselves to Him as we are. There is no room in a question of eternal life or eternal death for the courtesies of insincerity. The trees of the garden do not really hide us from our Creator's Eye; but they do enable us for a moment to practise on ourselves the paltry deceit of supposing that we escape Him. Let us look to it; that while time is still our own, and Eternity is still in the future, we walk forth, each as God calls, into the light of perfect truth,—the Truth of God's Awful Justice, but also the Truth of His Boundless Mercy—the Truth of our own special burden of sin and shame, but also the Truth and power of that Cleansing Blood which our Lord shed from His sacred Veins, that we might dare, even in our weakness, to be true, and that the Truth in its strength might make us free.

SERMON III.

GOD IN HIS REVEALED PERFECTIONS THE OBJECT OF WORSHIP.

BY

THE REV. T. L. CLAUGHTON, M.A.

HONORARY CANON OF WORCESTER,
AND VICAR OF KIDDERMINSTER.

SERMON III.

Ps. cxxx. 4.

There is forgiveness with Thee, that Thou mayest be feared.

In this Psalm, the sixth of those which are called Penitential Psalms, David pleads earnestly that deep want of the creature which the Creator alone can supply: in condescension to which indeed, God has been pleased to reveal Himself to our else confused and perplexed minds as a God of infinite mercy and love. He does not describe, as in some of the former Psalms of this character, the agonies of a wounded and contrite spirit; but he expresses in a few words that condition of our race into which the sin of our first parents has brought all their descendants, and which in every meditation on the character and attributes of God must be first taken into consideration: for we know nothing of God really except what He is to us: what He hath been pleased to reveal Himself to us in relation to those manifold wants and infirmities with which we find ourselves encompassed, the groanings and travailings of this fallen creation. From this point of view, to which a long and bitter experience has brought him, the Psalmist ascends to that view of the Divine perfections which the words of the text and other words which follow them contain, and which it will be my humble endeavour in this discourse to shew to be the true origin of all acceptable worship; the first spring of that affiance in God, which is the natural homage of our souls, when once we have discovered our true relation to one infinitely holy and good and pure as He. "Out of the depths have I cried unto Thee, O Lord;" so this beautiful Psalm begins: "Lord, hear my voice; let Thine ear be attentive to the voice of my supplication." "From the depths of sin," saith Bp. Horne, "and the misery occasioned by sin, the penitent, like another Jonas entombed in the whale's belly and surrounded by all the terrors of the ocean, crieth unto God for help. And we can scarce help being reminded by the words, of those prisoners of hope that yet lie in the grave—of the souls that cry, How long, O Lord, holy, just and true, before these longings shall be fulfilled, and the morning of the resurrection come?"

Then comes the first plea for mercy. "If Thou, Lord, shouldest mark iniquities, O Lord, who shall stand?" That we are but sinful dust and ashes, that our best doings are imperfect, that if God were to enter into judgment with us, we could not answer unto Him one charge in a thousand, has been the confession of all His saints and servants from the beginning. It is not merely the sense of His great power, His eternity and infinity, that awes us in our approaches to the place where His presence is: but it is the sense of our own unworthiness, and of the purity of Him with whom we have to do. It is still with us, as it was with our first parents when they hid themselves from the presence of the Lord God amongst the trees of the garden. We need something to cloke, to cover, to heal, to remedy our sin.

To this appointed remedy, or covering, the next words of the Psalmist direct us. "But there is forgiveness with Thee: therefore shalt Thou be feared." Yea, Thou hast devised means whereby Thy banished ones shall be brought back to Thee; as Thou spakest by the mouth of Elihu long before David's time, "I have found a ransom[1]." Yea, though "surely God will not do wickedly, neither will the Almighty

[1] Job xxxiii. 24.

pervert judgment[1]," yet hath He in a manner inscrutable to us made a way for His compassions to flow forth, even while "He shall render unto men according to their works, and cause every man to find according to His ways[1]." And here, brethren, lies the mysterious reason, why to beings constituted as we are, and placed in this world of trial and sorrow, the first among the Divine attributes is mercy. When Moses desired to see the glory of God, God answered his request, saying, "I will make my goodness pass before thee, and I will proclaim the name of the Lord before thee; and will be gracious to whom I will be gracious, and will shew mercy on whom I will shew mercy[2]." From which we are to learn that the especial glory of God is the sovereignty of His goodness: He doth indeed what He will with His own, and goodness is His own; it is His nature, His being. God is love. How can He choose but love, and shew mercy?

Indeed there is no limit to His mercy, but that which we ourselves by our perverseness interpose. As when He proclaimed His name unto Moses on Mount Sinai, after the declaration above referred to; He passed by before him, and proclaimed, "The Lord, The Lord God, merciful and gracious, longsuffering,

[1] Job xxxiv. 12. 11. [2] Exod. xxxiii. 19.

and abundant in goodness and truth, keeping mercy for thousands; forgiving iniquity and transgression and sin:"—then comes the limit, the only barrier and limit to the fulness and freeness of the Divine mercy—"and that will by no means clear the guilty." For this is another attribute of God—Justice. His mercy is of such a kind that it doth not interfere with the ordinary administration of Justice. Else mercy would be no more mercy, if it confounded right with wrong: yea, it is consistent with much severity of Justice; as the proclamation proceedeth to declare, "Visiting the iniquity of the fathers upon the children, unto the third and to the fourth generation[1]." The mercy of God is of such sort as to be consistent with the ordained consequences of sin described in these words; with the results that naturally flow out of it; as the transgression of a father doth almost necessarily impair the moral sense in his children, or tends to place them in circumstances most prejudicial to their spiritual progress, so that his iniquity is visited upon them in the way of a direct consequence. God's mercy is not the impulsive irregular mercy of an imperfect being; but the just and deeply-considered mercy of One whose knowledge embraces, whose power controls and regulates all causes, all effects;

[1] Exod. xxxiv. 6, 7.

so that all things shall work together for good to them that love God, to them who are the called according to His purpose. When He saith, "I will have mercy on whom I will have mercy"—into that "I will" enters the wisdom, the justice, and the power, of Him that willeth. He could not will against His own unerring wisdom, against His own impartial justice; or carry out by His sovereign power any sentence which was not just and wise, even as merciful. Yea, this is the key to the great mystery of godliness—God manifest in the flesh; the incarnation of our Lord Jesus Christ—not only that wisdom devised it, or that power achieved it, or that justice required it, but that mercy chose, willed, undertook, fulfilled it. He who was the brightness of the Father's glory, and the express image of His Person, must needs, by Himself, in the likeness of our flesh, purge our sins, ere he sat down triumphant on the right hand of the Majesty on High, having accomplished all His Father's will. The work was then finished in all its parts, when the Son of Man was glorified, and God was glorified in Him. Justice was satisfied. Wisdom was justified. The power of God had wrought a work worthy to be praised and had in honour, for which heaven should echo with joyful hallelujahs for ever and for evermore: as the Psalmist uttered it in song, "Mercy and truth are met together: righteousness and peace have kissed each other[1]." For so they did in the Atonement. There was "God in Christ reconciling the world unto Himself, not imputing their trespasses unto them[2]." And this is the special work which He hath commissioned us, as His ambassadors, to declare. He hath committed unto us the Word of Reconciliation. "Now then we are ambassadors for Christ, as though God did beseech you by us: we pray you, in Christ's stead, be ye reconciled to God[3]." Our mission is not so much to tell you that God alone doeth great wonders; or that by His wisdom He made the heavens; or executing justice, overthrew Pharaoh and his host in the Red Sea; though all this we may tell you as illustrating His mercy to His people—but we should ever say with David, "My song shall be always of the loving-kindness of the Lord, with my mouth will I ever be shewing Thy truth from one generation to another. For I have said, Mercy shall be built up for ever[4]."

The Prophets all with one consent confirm the teaching of David in the text, that it is forgiveness, the tender mercy and compassion of our God, for

[1] Ps. lxxxv. 10. [2] 2 Cor. v. 19.
[3] 2 Cor. v. 20. [4] Ps. lxxxix. 1, 2.

which He is feared and worshipped. "They shall fear the Lord and His goodness[1]," saith Hosea; fear Him, not with a slavish fear, which should make them turn away from His awful majesty; but with a reverent, holy fear, whereby they shall flee to Him for help, drawn by His Goodness, assured by His Love! And Micah to the same effect, "They shall be afraid of the Lord our God, and shall fear because of Thee. Who is a God like unto Thee, that pardoneth iniquity, and passeth by the transgression of the remnant of His heritage? He retaineth not His anger for ever, because He delighteth in mercy[2]." Yes, my brethren, we do not so much fear Him on account of His awful justice; or on account of His infinite power; or for His wisdom in ordering all things, as for His mercy, manifested unto us in the Son of His love: "We love Him, because He first loved us[3]." And this, brethren, is the true principle of worship. Yea, we know no other that can endure the test, or subdue in the heart of the worshipper that proneness to self-worship which is deep in every man's heart naturally, but this; this which rivets a man's whole soul on that which God has been to himself, a Saviour. What are the wonders of crea-

[1] Hosea iii. 5. [2] Micah vii. 17, 18.
[3] 1 John iv. 19.

tion, or the intricacies of Providence, to the mysteries of grace, to the mysterious union of justice and mercy, of wisdom and power, in the salvation of a sinful soul, and that soul mine,—my immortal part; yea, and if in other faculties with which God hath endowed me there be the instinct of immortality, as men are wont to anticipate the bursting in of new truth upon the intellect, after our transformation in death; how much stronger and clearer is that instinct in this part, the part in which all feeling resides, over which the sense of God's terror or displeasure exercises so strong an influence, and which is full of joyful anticipation of dwelling in His presence for ever, or shrinks in dread from the idea of being for ever in a state of banishment, separation, and loss! The very essence of worship is love in us, drawn forth by the sense of God's infinite love and mercy towards us in Jesus Christ our Lord. We fear Him or worship Him, as knowing that there is forgiveness with Him, and with Him alone; and so we worship Him most intensely when we stand, as it were, at the foot of the cross, to which He nailed the handwriting of ordinances that was against us[1], that must have condemned us, had He not taken it out of the way; or when we contemplate the tomb where His body was laid, empty now,

[1] Col. ii. 14.

for that He is risen, and lo! we with Him, by virtue of His resurrection, are "begotten again unto a lively hope[1]," and do the acts of a new life; or when we behold Him by faith, where St Stephen and St Paul saw Him with the fleshly eye standing at the right hand of God. Then we worship when we see and feel in all our hearts His goodness overflowing into beneficence and condescension and graciousness and mercy and forgiveness and joy in imparting Himself to those whose need He alone can supply, and complacence in the creatures He has formed and reformed, and redeemed and sanctified to His glory[2].

"But," says the unbeliever, "this is a carnal worship; you want nothing but the effigies of these things graven and fashioned before your eyes to make this absolute idolatry—mere worship of historical circumstances and events: we worship God abstractedly, understanding Him indeed 'by the things that are made, even His eternal power and Godhead[3],' and adoring that unseen essence whose greatness we thus apprehend; conceiving also how good He is by the works of Christ when He was upon the earth, by His life and death, according to the will of God. Such is our spiritual worship." But such a worshipper never saith unto the God whom

[1] 1 Pet. i. 3. [2] See Pusey on Hosea iii. 5.
[3] Rom. i. 20.

he worships, "There is forgiveness with thee, that thou mayest be feared." The mercy of God is not the object of his worship, but His wisdom, or His power, or His admirable adjustment of all parts of this outward universe; yea, of all its moral as well as its physical and material forces. Much there is of such imaginative worship in the world now; much that scarcely recognizes the personality of God as a Being of infinite Love and Purity, and which certainly does not realize that revealed relation to Him of which St Peter speaks in connection with the great and glorious promises of the Gospel; "by which," he says, "we become partakers of the divine nature, having escaped the corruption which is in the world through lust[1]." Our putting off as concerning the former conversation, the old man, which is corrupt according to the deceitful lusts; our being renewed in the spirit of our mind; our putting on the new man, which after God is created in righteousness and true holiness[2], is to one who does not really believe in the Atonement, or forgiveness, the mere preference of higher to lower pleasures, the mere natural result of intellectual development, which has lifted a man above viler concupiscences. But even if this were

[1] 2 Pet. i. 4. [2] Eph. iv. 22—24.

so, as such men profess, even if such a development, ever so highly advanced, did enable a man to "cleanse himself from all filthiness of flesh and spirit, and to perfect holiness in the fear of God[1]," where are those marks of the Lord Jesus which have been ever most conspicuous in the true worshippers; in the man after God's own heart; in them that have cried out in the pangs of a conscience convinced of sin, "Oh! wretched man that I am, who shall deliver me from the body of this death"? and then have made answer unto themselves by the power of faith uprising within them, "I thank God, through Jesus Christ our Lord[2]"? Where in such men is the ardent longing which David expresses, in the Psalm from which the text is taken, for the salvation of God: "I wait for the Lord, my soul doth wait for Him; and in His word do I hope. My soul waiteth for the Lord more than they that watch for the morning; I say, more than they that watch for the morning[3]"? The guards that hasten to their watches before the dawn are not earlier than I in my daily resort unto God. "Like as the hart desireth the waterbrooks, so longeth my soul after Thee, O God[4]." Where, in such men, is the constant, actual sense of God's presence described in those

[1] 2 Cor. vii. 1.
[2] Rom. vii. 25.
[3] Ps. cxxx. 5, 6.
[4] Ps. xlii. 1.

words, "I foresaw the Lord alway before me. He is on my right hand, therefore I shall not be moved[1]," accompanied with that confident expectation of "beholding His presence in righteousness;" of seeing Him as He is, when we awake up after His likeness? But, above all, where is the blissful sense of sharing these blessings with others—the true communion of saints—communion with all who are striving unto the same hope with ourselves, in holy worship; in the offering of the "sacrifice of praise to God continually, that is, the fruit of our lips giving thanks to His Name[2]"—where is the heart of man answering to the heart of his fellow-man in the noblest of all employments, in that which we learn from the Book of Revelation is to be the employment of angels and saints for ever? Where is this joy of Christian fellowship—the fellowship of believers with the Father, and with His Son Jesus Christ—the joy which tribulation makes more intense, because tribulation worketh endurance, and through much endurance the love of God is shed abroad in our hearts, as we read of Paul and Barnabas, that when the men of Antioch "raised persecution against them, and expelled them out of their coasts[3];" they "were filled

[1] Ps. xvi. 8.   [2] Heb. xiii. 15.
[3] Acts xiii. 50.

with joy, and with the Holy Ghost:" or as when afterward in Philippi, Paul and Silas, being thrust into the inner prison, with their feet made fast in the stocks, "prayed and sang praises unto God[1]"—worshipped the Great Sufferer, "rejoicing that they were counted worthy to suffer shame for His Name[2]"?

Brethren, of joys like these, those ideal worshippers of whom I spoke are not partakers, by the very nature of their idea of God. What their idea of God is, may be seen in their idea of what is most like Him in His creatures; for unto His image we all aspire. What they affect and seek is grandeur of thought, boldness of conception, depth of research, expansion of the mind by such researches; till it has acquired what is called a comprehensive view—a vigorous grasp—seeing what other men cannot see; having a deeper insight into mysteries than the ignorant and unenlightened have. But all this does not generate human sympathy, and least of all sympathy in worship: for in worship has been from the beginning the expression of a common want; the confession of a common sinfulness. All such ideas did our blessed Lord reject, when, perceiving at the very beginning of His ministry what a hindrance pride should be to the establishment of His spiritual

[1] Acts xvi. 25. [2] Acts v. 41.

kingdom, He said, "I thank Thee, O Father, Lord of heaven and earth, that thou hast hidden these things from the wise and prudent, and hast revealed them unto babes. Even so, Father: for so it seemed good in Thy sight[1]."

Brethren, the season reminds me that I may be addressing some who are even now preparing themselves for the ministry, to which St Paul counted it his greatest glory to have been called. You may not be called (though who can say you shall not) to endure such labours and sufferings as St Paul endured. But on some of you, surely, will devolve in due time the care of the churches, the duty of maintaining in its pureness and integrity the Faith of the Gospel. On some of those here present may depend in some critical conjuncture, as they shall stand fast or give way, the maintenance of some bulwark, against which the winds and storms of unbelief may be beating violently; or which vain deceivers may be persuading them, for peace sake and the ostensible promotion of charity, to surrender into their hands. It is impossible to forecast the manner of the assault, but the preparation for defence is plain: it is revealed in that word with which our Lord put to flight the tempter in his last assault upon His alle-

[1] Matt. xi. 25, 26.

giance, "Thou shalt worship the Lord thy God, and Him only shalt thou serve[1]." Yea, the last precept in the last prophetic book of the New Testament is the same. When St John, after beholding in vision the things which are to be hereafter, would have fallen down to worship before the feet of the Angel who shewed him these things, he received that check which is surely significant unto all time: "See thou do it not: for I am thy fellowservant, and of thy brethren the prophets, and of them which keep the sayings of this book: worship God[2]." Worship Him in His revealed perfections—worship Him as "He hath given you an understanding, that you may know Him that is true, and you are in Him that is true, even in His Son Jesus Christ: this is the true God, and eternal life[3]." Worship Him! Yea, and might we not add in the words next following, addressed by the same St John to his children in the faith, "Little children, keep yourselves from idols[4]." The Church in all ages has been tempted with idol worship, according to the corrupt tendencies of the heart, or the errors of the understanding. Let not the conceit of anything that is good in you, or the admiration of any man's person, or the doubts that are now sown

[1] Matt. iv. 10.
[2] Rev. xxii. 8, 9.
[3] 1 John v. 20.
[4] 1 John v. 21.

broadcast on every subject beyond the region of demonstration or experiment, ever lure you away from worshipping God according to the faith in which you have been brought up. "Let that abide in you which ye have heard from the beginning. If that which ye have heard from the beginning abide in you, ye also shall continue in the Son, and in the Father[1]."

We may live to see mighty changes, brethren, as those that come after us surely will: mighty changes—and yet the Eternal Truth through all these changes abiding still the same, as it is written "Jesus Christ the same yesterday, to-day, and for ever[2]." Ever the same Lord. Ever the one Faith. Ever the one Baptism. Ever the one God and Father of all, who is above all, and through all, and in all[3]. And this, however largely the Church may extend the bounds of her habitation. Every new mission that is opened; every tribe that is added to the fast multiplying tribes of the Lord; every prince among the heathen who becomes a worshipper of the true God, or sanctions that worship among his people; every convert who is baptized; every enquiry that is set on foot, every disputation that is

[1] 1 John ii. 24. [2] Heb. xiii. 8.
[3] Eph. iv. 4, 5.

held concerning His Name, which we know is to be magnified among the heathen; I might go further, and say,—every persecution that is endured; every adversary that is stirred up against the faith; the wrath and enmity of Satan as it spreads, are to us so many evidences of the power of God's grace, which when we see we rejoice and are glad, and feel that Christ is triumphing, and from His seat at God's right hand expecting till, one by one, every foe shall be subdued under His feet, and His kingdom established over all.

SERMON IV.

ABRAHAM STANDING BEFORE THE LORD.

BY

THE REV. J. R. WOODFORD, M.A.

VICAR OF KEMPSFORD,
AND EXAMINING CHAPLAIN TO THE LORD BISHOP OF OXFORD.

SERMON IV.

GENESIS XVIII. 22.

But Abraham stood yet before the Lord.

THE position of Abraham in the history of God's dealings with our race is a very remarkable one. It is not only that he is the ancestor of that peculiar people, whose annals are the annals of true religion: Abraham is the first member of the Church in the fulness of its visibility. In him we might almost say began that vast company of believers who, gathered out of the world, have lived in public and confessed covenant with God. The Creator had His saints before Abraham, but they were rather isolated examples of individual sanctity. When Abraham was called; when in the far wilds of Mesopotamia the Lord God (how we know not) appeared unto him and bade him go forth from his father's house, the great line of demarcation between the visible Church and the rest of the world was finally drawn. The journey of the patriarch to the Euphrates and beyond its mysterious waters, is the journey of the Church of God, out into the world it was to leaven and civilize. As the full harvest is in the seed, so in the tent of the patriarch was hidden the universal Church hereafter to overshadow the earth.

Hence the deep interest which attaches to the patriarchal period, because in it is the germ of our own ecclesiastical life. Thus, circumcision is to be regarded not only as the distinctive mark of a race, but as the first expression of that great law of grace under which God has been pleased to deal with men's souls, through all time; the sacramental law by which things outward, visible, in themselves insignificant, are made the vehicles of salvation, the pledge of present and future blessing.

So again the sacrifice of Isaac stands out, not as a strange command by which God was pleased arbitrarily to prove the obedience of His servant, but a revelation, at the moment when the Church was first severed from the world, of the transcendant mystery which the Church was constituted to enshrine, the mystery of a Father giving His only Son to be a sacrifice and oblation. Realize the position of Abraham as the first of the visible Church, and half the difficulties about the offering of Isaac vanish. It is then seen to have a wonderful propriety in time and circumstance. The probation of Abraham's faith was but an incidental good, secondary to the higher purpose of giving him to see for one moment into the depths of the secret of the Lord. "Your father Abraham—it is Christ's own commentary in all likelihood upon this very event—rejoiced to see my day: he saw it and was glad."

So, once more, with regard to the worship of God, of which we are to speak to-day. In the twilight of far ages an old man cometh up. From spot to spot on the borders of the remotest East I behold him moving to and fro, and ever as he reaches a fresh halting-place he builds up his altar and sacrifices to his God—on the plain of Moreh, on the mountain east of Bethel, amid the oaks of Mamre; and, lo! it is no self-taught homage of a rude Arab chief to a divinity equally rude which I behold. The faith of that man is our faith; the hope of that man is our hope. The worship of that man is the divinely-taught worship of the Church of God in its earliest developement. In his unceasing remembrance of the nearness of the Invisible; in the devout setting apart wherever he tarries of a place on which he may stand before the Lord; in that repeated altar-raising, which he can never afterwards have shared in without thrilling at the memory of the scene on Mount Moriah; the fire and the wood and one in the form of man bound thereupon; the majestic image of the great patriarch stands out in the dim distance the teacher of covenant-worship to the universal Church to the end. Come then, let us sit a little while at his feet, and by the altar of Abraham look into some of the features of all true and reasonable worship of God.

I. And first with regard to worship as involving prayer to God.

Now we shall not be going too far in saying that the common idea of prayer, if men were to speak out their opinions, would be found to be that it is a devotional exercise by which the spiritual part of our being is cultivated and improved. Prayer is with most people a pious duty, not a motive power. Those who are most regular in praying scarcely look for any direct result from their prayers: they regard worship as a thing which acts upon themselves, not upon God. The solemn litany elevates and chastens their own mind: they hardly expect it to have any effect upon the course of events. To this non-realization of prayer, as that which in the bold words of the old writer "vanquishes God," may be attributed the coldness and indifference with which men pray.

If they felt that the words whispered below surely and indeed mounted upward, that they were gifted with a power upon the wheels of the universe, think you not the voice of supplication would swell out with mightier tone, and the wave of national and individual devotion heave upwards with a stronger impulse? And to what are we to trace this habit of regarding prayer as an agent for improving man, rather than of influencing God? Must we not, if we are candid, confess that it arises out of our tendency to substitute general laws as guiding the world in the place of a personal God? The low estimate of prayer lands you, if you carry out the principle, in Atheism.

Now, the text, representing Abraham in the act of intercession, gives very impressively the counter-view to this. It introduces that marvellous history of the importunate pleading of the Patriarch for Sodom. The mysterious visitants, in entertaining whom, St Paul says that he entertained angels, had gone on their road to the doomed cities of the plain. "The men," it is said, "turned their faces from thence and went towards Sodom: but Abraham stood yet before the Lord." The expression probably is to be classed with other expressions which seem to indicate that even in that early period, and notwithstanding his migratory life, the Patriarch had a fixed spot adjoining his temporary settlement for acts of worship. The language is akin to that in which it is written, that "Abraham drew near and said"—"that he gat up early in the morning to the place where he stood before the Lord;" "that Isaac expressed a desire to bless his favourite son, "before the Lord." In all these passages it is probable that the phrase, "before the Lord," indicates primarily the place where prayer was wont to be made. But yet we may not ignore the feeling manifested in the very originating of the phrase, viz. the possibility of an approach to a Personal God.

Two convictions about God are prominent in the whole history of Abraham, convictions which lie at the root of all real worship. There is, first, his vivid realization of God as the Ruler of Nature. See this in his constant reference of temporal blessings to God personally manifested, "The Lord appeared unto Abraham, and said, Unto thy seed will I give this land: and there builded he an altar unto the Lord who appeared unto him." So in that wonderful vision recorded in Gen. xv., where the Lord is said to have brought Abraham forth abroad and pointed to the stars of heaven as a picture of what his posterity should be, that which in this and the like passages comes so sharply into view is the felt action of a Divine Person, willing, moderating, guiding, the destinies of the worshipper and his seed; the giver of territory, the multiplier of offspring, the dispenser of bondage and deliverance. Nothing seems to happen by what we call "Law," but the whole, the great and the small, to be the result of the Personal Will of a manifested God.

The second point to be noticed is the intense conviction in Abraham's mind of having been brought into peculiar relations to God. It is visible in the determination with which he holds aloof from the people of the land in which he dwells, his profession of being a stranger among them, his dread of any alliance by marriage with them, his otherwise unaccountable refusal, at a time when his heart was most softened by the death of Sarah, to accept as a gift the cave of Machpelah. He would not be indebted to the kindly Ephron even for a resting-place for his dead. We know not of any satisfactory explanation of this part of the narrative save that which is to be found in the deep-rooted conviction of having been separated from the outer world, and brought into special relations with the Almighty[1].

[1] It has been pointed out to the author since this sermon was preached, that it is probably wrong to find in Ephron's language the *bonâ fide* offer of a friend. It is said to be still the custom in the East that when a stranger asks the price of an article, the eager salesman

Now these two principles must underlie all prayer that is not an utter unreality. Whilst the hopefulness of prayer hinges in no small degree upon our being constituted as Christians into the family of God, and so privileged to address Him in a truer sense than any part of the human race, as "Our Father, which art in heaven," the reasonableness of praying at all depends upon the course of nature and of grace being ordered by the Personal Will of God. Take the case of temporal blessings. In proportion to your confidence that prudence and energy can of themselves command success, will be your apathy in applying for help to another Being. Once let the notion insinuate itself that all things on earth proceed according to a fixed, absolute, unchangeable law, which allows no scope for the intervention of a Personal Will; that this law is inherent in the nature of things, or has been set once for all in the beginning, and it will be very difficult to pray with

politely offers it to him as a present. If accepted, a present in return of at least equal value is expected. But the buyer in his turn politely thanks the other for his gracious offer and begs as a favour to know the value. A depreciating answer is made, whilst a sum is at the same time named beyond the real value. Upon this the wrangling begins and the sale is concluded for less than half the price named. Abraham avoided the dispute by at once paying to Ephron the sum of money first demanded.

The view in the text appears to be that taken by Dean Milman. Vid. *Hist. of the Jews*, Vol. I. p. 25.

any expectation of results; and the moment you cease to look for results, the soul of prayer is gone. So with spiritual things. It may be quite true that certain sins spring out of certain natural temperaments; that some by coldness of constitution are spared trials under which others fall; that unbelief itself is the result of a mental constitution. The acceptance of such theory as the whole truth is fatal to any hearty prayer for divine succour or enlightenment.

It is hard, nay, it is perhaps impossible, for us to reconcile the action of a personal will in God with those laws of the moral universe to which we cannot blind ourselves: hard for us to imagine a change in the purposes of one who knows all things long before, consequent upon the intercession of the creature. But it is the grand theme of the Bible, this exhibition of the world, moral and physical, as ruled by the hand of a Divine Person, doing according to His pleasure in the hosts of heaven and the armies of hell. It is here as in other points. Science and inspiration bring out two aspects of truth. We may not now be able to harmonize them,—we are to accept. both, and wait for their reconcilement. Thus philosophy brings us in contact with "Law" as pervading the universe, Inspiration unveils to us One above law, whose bosom is the seat of law, the Almighty God acting according to His arbitrary will; and it grounds upon this truth the injunction to "Pray." And just in proportion as we give this truth of inspiration its due place in our hearts, in proportion as through the ravelled web of cause and effect we see One sitting on His throne, will our prayers be warm or lifeless, fervent or dull.

Here then is the first point which we would press home. If there is to be prayer, prayer not as a form, not as a pious exercise in which the mind meditates upon solemn verities, but prayer, as the Bible describes it, having power with God; then, in the language of St Paul (and that language, you will see, goes very deep) must you believe that "He is," not an abstraction, not a law, but what we most nearly express by the word "Person," then must you feel with Abraham, that when you pray you draw near; then must you have clearly before your soul, as he had, "a God that has appeared." Aye, that first manifestation of the Almighty, when He dwelt beyond the flood, was the key-stone of his life. As with St Paul in later days, so with the Patriarch, the shining of that unearthly light in which God was, never faded out from his gaze. The voice which he had heard never ceased to thrill in his ear. Behind the screen of the visible dwelt (as he was abidingly conscious) One unseen. So when he prayed, it was not to discipline his own soul, not to cherish in himself a higher life. He did not look inward, but without, when he lifted up his hands, for the result of his worship: for to him worship was in no figure of speech, but in very truth "a standing before the Lord."

II. But worship comprehends thanksgiving for past mercies, as well as prayer for future blessings. Let us turn to this aspect of the subject.

We have spoken of the reality of prayer depending upon a vivid realization of God, not as an abstract power, but as a person ordering all things according to His will. It is to be feared that this conception of the Almighty is one which is imperceptibly weakening. We cannot but think that not only the coldness of our prayers, but many difficulties on religious points which now agitate reflecting minds, have their root in an obscure perception of God as a Divine Person. For example, the whole subject of miracles. Surely the difficulty which some men find in accepting the truth of "miracles," if you trace it to its source, lies here, that they have come to forget God as a Living Agent in the march of human life. They have so exaggerated the one truth, that the course of nature is regulated by general laws imposed long ago, as to forget the fellow-truth, that the continual working of those laws is under the superintendence of a Supreme Will. And it is in the fact of a Living God, whose will is above law, that the possibility of miracles is grounded. If in your mind's vision the Eternal God withdraws, as it were, into an impersonal abstraction, the difficulty of recognising any variation in the ordinary course of events forthwith enlarges.

Take, again, the question of "inspiration." The exact nature of inspiration—how the divine afflatus acted in the prophet or evangelist—whether as a wholly new power, or as a quickening and strengthening only of the natural capacities, the degree in which the man's own mind and ideas are to be detected in his writings, are all points of absorbing interest, upon which we naturally are eager to ascertain rules. But now again, does not the probability that any general rule exists, depend greatly upon the degree in which we realize the giver of inspiration as a Divine Person, in this as in other things, acting continuously according to His pleasure? What, after all, if there be no "law of inspiration"? if the mysterious gift be different in every author of the sacred books? This is unlikely if God be only the name of a power in the creation of grace—it is not unlikely, if

He be a person acting by His will. Recognize the Holy Ghost as the "Lord of life," supreme and uncontrolled in the substance and the manner of His gifts, and the likelihood of our being able to systematize a theory of inspiration becomes less.

And similarly, right conceptions of God as a Divine Person are, you will find closely bound up with the subject of "thanksgiving" in Divine worship. "I saw the Lord sitting on His throne, and His train filled the temple." If prayer must wither and die as soon as that vision of a reigning Lord and His thousand ministers fades out from the soul's gaze, thanksgiving can have no existence at all. Gratitude is from a person to a person—as it springs up only in a living heart, so must it have for its object a living Being. It is only by a figure of speech that you can talk of being grateful to an order, or a rule: gratitude involves the emotions of love, the desire of pleasing, the wish to recompense, and those emotions cannot flow save towards a personal friend: so long as you see God dimly, you must needs love God coldly. And hence perhaps the reason why even great saints are often less earnest in thanksgiving than in prayer; and why, on the other hand, the Bible never speaks of the prayers of angels, but only of their everlasting song. It is as though earth were the footstool of prayer, and the heavenly sanctuary the great theatre of praise. And wherefore? Ah, may not the reason be in the fact that here we see through a glass darkly; there, face to face. Here a hundred mediate agencies intervene between us and the hand of God; there they receive directly out of His fulness. It is this close immediate action of God in heaven which is expressed in all those passages: "God shall wipe away all tears from their eyes." "The Lamb that is in the midst of the throne shall feed them." And simultaneously with that near vision of the eternal King, the grand outburst of praise begins. It is the sight of God which kindles the creature into love, and wakens the hallelujah which never dies.

Yea, and thanksgiving is something greater still. They take a low view of praise who limit it only to the tribute of the creature for personal benefits. What is the meaning of those words in our eucharistic hymn, "We give thanks to Thee for Thy great glory"? Not for what God has done, but for what He is, is the voice of praise uplifted. Is it not the faint struggle of the earthly congregation to catch for one moment, when freshly fed with the bread of heaven, the intense worship of the mighty company above? But here, again, we need hardly stay to argue, the whole edifice of such praise is founded upon the sense of One high and lifted up, One who is not law but the Giver of law, not order but the Creator of order, not creation but the Builder of the Universe.

And so, men and brethren, whether you regard worship as a thing of prayer or of praise, you may go back to the old patriarch as its type: "Abraham stood yet before the Lord." These few words ring out the true note of all prayer and thanksgiving. You may explain them away if you will, as intended only to denote that he stood still in the place of prayer, but indeed, places of prayer, our churches and our sanctuaries, have for their fundamental idea the mighty verity, that God liveth, and may, in no figure of speech but in sober reality, be approached unto. Would ye learn to pray with the spirit and the understanding also, with the warm feelings of the heart, and the homage of the intellect; would ye try (all feebly and faulty it needs must be) the notes of that eternal song which rings for ever through the house not made with hands; would ye take from your devotions all that weariness and dullness which now hangs about them, and turn them from being a mere perfunctory discharge of an unwelcome duty into the joyous communings of spirit with spirit, mind with mind, then must you shake yourselves free from those vague philosophies which have well-nigh banished God from His own creation, and realize yourselves in the hour of worship, as appearing before that Divine Person who worketh on every side, yet whose veil none have lifted, and so in very truth standing before the Lord.

And now but a few words in conclusion.

The essence of worship is the consciousness and recognition of God. With a vague perception of God, your prayers and praises must alike be cold and dull. Contrariwise, the neglect of prayer and praise is the beginning of unbelief. If you pray irregularly, sometimes omitting altogether, sometimes hurrying over your morning and evening prayers, you undermine your own belief. So again, do not be tempted to philosophize away the true idea of worship. Worship is the bodily and mental adoration of the Lord, the kneeling knee and the uplifted voice are essential elements of worship. Never let these slip under a veil of mysticism and poetry, as though beautiful thoughts, or an admiration of nature, would stand instead of definite acts of prayer and praise.

Worship,—it is the creature gathering up deliberately, consciously, all his faculties of body and soul in the presence of the Creator, calling in all his wondrous gifts, thought, memory, imagination, fear, awe, love, and so, with his whole being concentrated on one object, standing before the Lord.

SERMON V.

GOD FASHIONING THE HEARTS OF HIS PEOPLE.

BY

EDWARD MEYRICK GOULBURN, D.D.

PREBENDARY OF ST PAUL'S,
CHAPLAIN OF THE BISHOP OF OXFORD,
AND ONE OF HER MAJESTY'S CHAPLAINS IN ORDINARY.

SERMON V.

ROM. VIII. 29.

Whom He did foreknow, He also did predestinate to be conformed to the image of His Son, that He might be the firstborn among many brethren.

IN the fine Arts there are two sorts of products of Human Industry. We may make an original; or we may make a copy. In making an original, the mind of the artist conceives the idea, and then his hand works up to its realisation. In making a copy, his eye does what his mind did in making the original: he places his model before him; his picture or his statue is to be as like that model as may be; and he is continually fastening his eye upon the model, and guiding his hand accordingly. He works not after an ideal, but after an object external to his mind.

One great truth brought before us in the passage I have read is that Almighty God, in fashioning the hearts of His people, works after a model, aims at producing not an original, but a copy. He predestinates us to be conformed to the Image of His Son. It is not by the abstract conception of virtue in the Divine Mind that the Holy Spirit regulates His hand; He has a realised ideal before Him in the perfect Humanity of Our Lord. And so far as our own will has an agency in the work of our sanctification (as of course it has) we are to set before us for our imitation the same great model, and never for a moment to work independently of it. St Paul, after giving certain abstract precepts for humility and unselfishness, seems to be struck with the thought of the feebleness of such precepts, as compared with the force and significance of the great Example; and accordingly says with emphasis, as if the whole compass of Christian duty were summed up in such an exhortation,—"Let *this* mind be in you which was also in Christ Jesus." And in another Epistle, he gives this account of the principle on which the sanctification of Christians proceeds: "We all, with open face beholding as in a glass the glory of the Lord, are changed into the same Image from glory to glory, even as by the Spirit of the Lord."

We shall speak to you then this evening on the subject which has been thus opened, the operations of Divine Grace upon Human Character, or (which appears, from what has been already said, to be the same thing) the formation of the character of Christ in the hearts of His disciples.

In order to the thorough sifting of the subject, one or two preliminary remarks are necessary on the different meanings attached to the word "character." Equivocal words which have more than one meaning (especially if the meanings are nearly allied) are a fertile source of confusion of thought. Thus it is with the word "character." Sometimes it is used in a *purely* moral sense, and denotes the will, habits, moral sentiments of a man, according as they are good or bad. Thus we say of one man that he bears a good character, of another that he has but an indifferent character, of a third that his character, though plausible, has no principle in it, and so forth. In short, in this sense of the word character, a man bearing the character is either good or bad. But the same word is used in another sense, which we must take care to discriminate, of the prevailing bias of sentiments, views, and tastes, with which we are born, and which, whatever moral changes we may undergo, accompanies us to the grave. Thus we speak of one man as a contemplative character, of another as an eminently practical character, of a third as a cold and phlegmatic, of a fourth as an ardent and genial character. We imply no blame, nor necessarily any praise, when we speak of them thus. They were born so; and they are not answerable for natural temperament. We may indeed imply a personal preference or dislike for them; but that is a distinct thing from moral censure or approbation.

Now in the first sense of the word character, God's people are all uniform in character, and ever tending to a still closer uniformity, being all conformed to the Image of His Son. In the second sense of the word character, there are infinite varieties among them, each one bringing out into prominence some one distinct feature of the mind of Him, who in His perfect Humanity, represents them all. Here therefore among the saints of God, who are His handiwork in Grace, you see traces of the same Law which regulates His Hand in Nature—Unity in Variety.

These then will be the two great divisions of our subject;

I. The uniformity of the operations of Grace in the heart of God's people, in virtue of their being all conformed to one Image,—"the Image of His Son."

II. The variety of the operations of Grace in the hearts of God's people, in virtue of their each bringing out in relief some one feature of that Image.

Character, according to the first sense of it, may be said to stand in the will, embracing under that term the various influences which determine the will. If it be asked in what Sanctity really consists, it must be answered, In the conformity of the human will to the Will of God. The definition, though short, is adequate. For our will is determined by, and moves in accordance with, our affections; so that for the human will to choose the Will of God implies that the affections and desires embrace that higher Will. And that the affections and desires should embrace God's Will with full consent is in other words to love the Lord our God. And the Love of God is the first and great commandment of the Law, and the chief constituent of all Sanctity.

Sanctity then consisting in the conformity of the human to the Divine Will, Sanctification, which is the production of Sanctity in the heart, must consist in bringing about that conformity.

Now, to speak first of the model which God proposes to Himself in fashioning the hearts of His people, what do we read in Holy Scripture respecting the Will of Christ and the operations upon His Will?

As regards the active fulfilment of the work which

God had given Him to do, we hear Him saying, "My meat is to do the will of Him that sent me, and to finish His work." "My meat is to do it." The soul of Christ hungered after the fulfilment of His task; there was a void in His heart, so long as there was work to be done for God, which was not yet done. And in doing this work, He experienced a positive and high satisfaction, analogous to the gratification of the bodily appetite when hunger is appeased. There was in His human heart a burning irrepressible energy to save human souls, to procure honour to God,—in short, to do everything which had been prescribed for Him in the counsels of Eternity, according to that other word of His: "I have a baptism to be baptized with, and how am I straitened till it be accomplished."

And the mention of this Baptism (which was one of suffering) calls our thoughts to another point. There is a Will of God which has to be actively carried into effect by us. And there is another Will of God which has to be passively endured. By loving zeal we throw ourselves into the first. By resignation we embrace the second. And what says Holy Scripture of resignation on the part of our Lord? Its teaching on this deep subject requires a few words of expansion and developement. Being made like unto us in all things, sin only excepted, our Lord shrank from pain and suffering in every shape as sensitively as we do. Shall I say that He shrank from it more sensitively? I believe it was so. There must have been in Him, in virtue of His immaculate purity, sensibilities which, if they exist at all in us, exist in a very low degree. How must sin have jarred upon the mind of One, who always retained the lively reminiscence of the glory which He had with the Father before the world was! And sorrow, suffering, and death would necessarily be viewed by Him (as they are scarcely ever viewed by us) in their living relation to sin,—viewed as so many poisonous fungus growths, which had sprung up from the moral rottenness of man's heart. Taking therefore a far deeper view of Suffering and Death than we can ever take, He would shudder with proportional intensity at its approach. And the more He shuddered, the more difficult would the task of resignation become. A glimpse is given us of His flesh (or lower will) declining the frightful ordeal to which the Father had called Him, in St Matthew's account of the Agony in the Garden. The first strong cry which He utters, in a momentary recoil from the powers of darkness which beset Him round about, is an actual petition for the removal of the

Cup: "O my Father, if it be possible, let this cup pass from Me: nevertheless not as I will, but as Thou wilt." But the second cry is differently worded. In the interval, the lower will, which declined pain and suffering, has been brought round into acquiescence with the higher, which embraced this pain and suffering as the Father's appointment, as the Law, under which alone Human Redemption could be wrought out. "O my Father, if this cup may not pass away from me, except I drink it, thy Will be done." The Apostle to the Hebrews thus strikingly comments upon this growing acquiescence of our Lord in His Father's Will; "Though He were a Son, yet learned He obedience by the things that He suffered." Obedience here means obedience to God in His orderings or arrangements, in other words, submission. This submission, we are told, our Blessed Lord condescended to learn amid the experience of bitter sufferings. The will of His human soul recalcitrated for an instant at the thought of the identification with sin and its curse which awaited Him. There was no sin whatever in this recalcitration. It was an instinct of Humanity. Humanity, though never so pure, must by the law of its being shrink from pain. Christ would not have been perfect man without this shrinking. And He would not have been our great model of resignation to the Father's appointments, had not the Holy Spirit in His human soul brought round this will of the flesh to yield itself up meekly to the higher will of the spirit.

These points of character, then,—zealous loving devotion to our Father's Will, when it prescribes our work,—meek resignation to it, when it appoints for us suffering—the Holy Spirit is continually reproducing in the hearts of God's people. I would remark that in a genuine work of Grace both will be found (sooner or later) together. We often see men throwing themselves with zeal, and not without a certain amount of religious principle, into their vocation, who are drawn to do so not so much by loving devotion to God's Will, as by the brightness and healthiness which activity of any kind naturally gives to the mind. Affliction explores the ground of the heart of such men. How is it with them, when they are laid by—laid, it may be, on a bed of languishing and pain? Can they then say,

> O Lord my God, do Thou Thy holy Will—
> I will lie still—
> I will not stir, lest I forsake Thine arm,
> And break the charm,
> Which lulls me, clinging to my Father's breast,
> In perfect rest.

Devotion to God's will, whether it prescribe action

or suffering, is the family likeness to the Head of the House, in which all the brotherhood of the Son of God are fashioned again. It is God's work this fashioning, in its beginning, progress, and end; for we are told that "it is God which worketh in us both to will and to do of His good pleasure." And in acknowledgement of our dependence upon Him for this Divine transformation of character, we must be earnest in prayer for it. Feeling our own powerlessness, except in subordination to and co-operation with His sovereign agency, we must present ourselves continually before Him, as a block of stone is laid before the sculptor, beseeching Him that He would put forth His hand and make us all that He approves, fashioning us after the Image of His dear Son.

But prayer alone, without a sincere endeavour to co-operate with the Heavenly Workman, will not attain the end. And it is a great point to see in what shape this endeavour should be made. Children are said in some cases to acquire a resemblance to the features (as we know they do to the manners) of those with whom they are familiarly conversant from their earliest years. Wild animals in high latitudes, which traverse a wilderness of snow, become white from looking at the snow. And there is a similar law in spiritual things, by which we are transformed into the resemblance of that, which we habitually look upon. "We all," says the Apostle Paul, "beholding as in a glass the glory of the Lord, are changed into the same image." "We know," says the Apostle John, "that when He shall appear, we shall be like Him; for we shall see Him as He is," and the seeing Him as He is will necessarily make our faces shine with the lustre of His Glory, as the face of Moses shone during his communion with God upon the Mount. This last passage refers to our future vision of Christ in glory. But the principle of our transformation in glory hereafter is the same as that of our present transformation in grace. In both cases transformation results from stedfastly gazing upon the Image. We have a perfect portraiture of our Blessed Lord's character, of His ardent zeal, of His beautiful resignation, in the Gospel Narratives. Let us constantly gaze upon this portraiture. Let us revolve much in our minds the human character of the Son of God. Let us strive to image to ourselves in a lively way what manner of man He was. Let us seek to live with Him in thought. And at this season more especially let us set ourselves to contemplate the moving scenes of His Passion, and watch the lamb-like submissiveness with which He surrenders Himself to the Ordination of God for Him in the volume of the Book, and to the cruelty of His enemies. So His Blessed likeness will grow upon us without further effort on our part. The lineaments of His resignation will be formed in our souls: "Beholding as in a glass the glory of the Lord, we shall be changed into the same image from glory to glory, even as by the Spirit of the Lord."

II. We now turn to the second part of our subject, the variety of the operations of Grace in the hearts of God's people, in virtue of their each bringing out in relief some one feature of Christ's Image.

Using the term "character" in the sense of predominating natural bias, it cannot but strike us how totally different are the characters of the Scriptural Saints. St John, for example, and St Paul. What two dispositions can exhibit greater differences? The first contemplative, a lover of seclusion, a character generally abhorrent of abrupt transitions, a character of deep spiritual growth rather than of external activity. St Paul, on the other hand, a man whose almost superhuman activities vibrate in the Church at the present day (we Gentiles being all his spiritual offspring, and the Reformation itself being mainly due to the revival of the influence of his writings), a man converted not by any gradual process of thought, but in a moment of time, a man with an impetuous will which carried along with it all wills of lesser calibre, much as the draught of a fire in some baronial hall catches up and whirls along with it feathers, and paper, and all light substances. St Peter again,—what a different type of character from either St John or St Paul! Warm and vehement in his attachments, with much of impulse, but not corresponding stedfastness, and therefore not always to be depended upon, a lover of all old associations, and therefore having a strong and somewhat narrow predilection for the Law, under which he had been born and bred. St James the Just, another type still! The devout man according to the strict legal view of devotion, one of antidogmatic turn of mind, who naturally conceives works of charity and piety to be the main substance of religion, who is reserved in speaking about doctrines and especially the doctrines of Grace, as feeling that all speech implies profession, and that all profession is hypocrisy without corresponding practice. Surely it cannot be without purpose that God has exhibited to us in the small compass of the New Testament four characters of His most eminent servants with differences so very marked. All these men were conformed (as regards the will and the affections) to the Image of their Master; yet the complexion of Sanctity in each seems to differ, from their exceedingly different natural temperament. There is indeed the one Light of the Mind of Christ streaming through each character; but as the one sunlight takes a tinge from the colour of the glass through which it passes, so this Mind of Christ exhibits itself in each in such a form as we might expect from the natural bent of the disposition.

This observation naturally leads us on to the enquiry: "What constitutes a perfect natural character, in the sense in which the term character is now being applied?" And the answer is, a thoroughly well-balanced character would be a perfect one. Thoughtfulness and a contemplative habit is an excellence. Practical energy is another excellence. Reserve certainly has its good points, and is valuable, when it does not pass into want of sympathy. Sympathy also, and a genial freedom in communicating our thoughts and sentiments, is a valuable trait. Impulsiveness in taking in hand an enterprise is good as a propelling force. But consistency and perseverance are no less necessary to success. Sanguineness helps us over difficulties, and gives generally a bright view of life; but caution and prudence are a necessary counterpoise to excessive sanguineness. The misfortune is, that in no mere man do we find these various elements of character compounded in the right measure. By character is usually meant the predominance of one or two elements over the others. The very predominance however is an imperfection. In a perfect character all the ingredients would be mixed together in due proportion; and there would be no exaggeration of any particular feature. We may employ an illustration to convey the truth more clearly. The light of the Sun, when analysed, is seen to contain in it all the colours which deck the face of nature. But none of the colours preponderates. They are all so beautifully tempered together that no one of them appears in the whole effect. The light is colourless, though it contains rays of indigo, of violet, of orange. Similarly, a perfect natural character would contain indeed every excellence, but have no predominating feature; He who possessed it would seem to be without a character; and yet, when any particular excellence was named, He would be recognised as exhibiting it. Was there ever then, a perfect natural character among men? We believe that our Blessed Lord is the only instance of such a character. We believe that, if you should read through the Gospels with the view of forming as definite an idea as might be of His human mind, you would come to just this conclusion; "No "excellence is absent; and yet He cannot be cha-"racterised by any single one." Was he contemplative? Deeply so. He spent whole nights in prayer. He lived alone with God in a lofty loneliness of thought, which none of His disciples could approach or understand. Yet to call Him contemplative by no means adequately describes Him. There never was among the children of men such an exhibition of stirring practical energy; from morning to night He was thronged by multitudes, who came to hear Him and to be healed of their diseases; and not even after the most fatiguing day would He deny them, or send them away empty. Was He sympathetic? His whole mission was but one continuous manifestation of His deep sympathy; and on those who acknowledged Him, when He was about to leave them, He poured out such a flood of tenderness, that in point of mere pathos, no human farewells have ever matched His parting discourses. "Greater love hath no man than this, that a man lay down his life for his friends." "Henceforth I call you not servants; for the servant knoweth not what his lord doeth; but I have called you friends: for all things that I have heard of my Father I have made known unto you." And yet this tender sympathy was marred by no weakness; it never degenerated into fond indulgence. How sternly did He turn upon Simon Peter, when urged by him to consult His own ease, rather than the eternal interests of souls! How sharply did He reprimand the beloved disciple and his brother, when they momentarily harboured a thought of revenge upon inhospitable Samaritans! How did He continually upbraid all His disciples with unbelief, slowness of apprehension, hardness of heart!—Was our Lord in favour of a free religion, independent of local associations, and prescribed ceremonial? It was He from whose lips first fell the sublime announcement; "Ye shall neither in this mountain, nor yet at Jerusalem, worship the Father. God is a Spirit: and they that worship Him must worship Him in spirit and in truth." And yet, on the other hand, was He not a lover of sacred associations, a devout frequenter of Holy Places, a scrupulous observer of prescribed forms? Eminently so. His anger (which usually slumbered) was roused by the desecration of His Father's house; He visited that sin, not with censure only, but with stripes; He regarded the Temple as a House; He resorted constantly to the synagogue; He would not exempt restored lepers from the legal offering binding upon them; nor even Himself from the payment of the Temple tax. In a word, there was in Him every excellence of natural character, without a predominance of any one. In all His saints natural character is only fragmentary—represents only one or two of the graces, which in Him were all exhibited in the most attractive harmony.

Then what practical use can we make of this latter part of the subject? We have seen that, in regard of the will, and the moral powers which influence the will, the members of the mystical Body of Christ are all conformed to the Head. But because each of these members has a certain mental temperament peculiarly his own, each will exhibit the Life which is in Christ after a different form. This then is to be borne in mind, and acquiesced in as the appointment of God for His Church. We must not even strive to cast Peter, Paul, and John into one mould of natural character; but rather be thankful for the instructive difference of shape in which each one of them exemplifies the spirit and principles of his Master. And for our own personal guidance and self-discipline, what help may we borrow from what has been said? It is remarkable how many a Christian, sincerely in pursuit of holiness, seems to fail and come short of the mark, for want of point to his endeavours. The energies of the will are dissipated by being spread over the whole area of Christian life; there is no definite aim round which all efforts may rally. Now might we not advantageously consult our own natural bias (ascertained by a serious and sifting self-examination) as to the form which in us the Life of Christ is meant to take? Perhaps the form is external activity; we may possibly have those gifts of strong will and genial sympathy which, wherever they exist, command influence with others. Then let us set ourselves, as our one object of Christian endeavour, to enlarge this influence and to exert it uniformly for Christ in the organization, administration, or active support of Charitable or Religious Institutions. Perhaps we are unfitted naturally for practical life, are students by predilection, apt rather to forge thoughts in the workshop of our own mind than to bring them to bear forcibly upon the minds of others. Then it becomes suitable to surrender a considerable portion of time to devotional exercises; to make secret communion with God and Christ something of a study; and to endeavour after usefulness to the Church, in the vast and varied field of Christian Literature. Perhaps our natural bias may be such that Religion must always take with us more or less the shape of Duty. I am not for a moment saying that in this case we may lawfully allow ourselves to regard the Gospel merely as a moral code,—still less, that we should not aim at correcting our natural onesidedness by the devout study of those Evangelical Doctrines, which are the very lifeblood of Christian practice. But I say that this habit of mind was the mould in which the piety of St James seem to have been cast; and that therefore modern piety may legitimately be cast into the same mould, and be no less acceptable to God through Christ, and perhaps may do no less service in the Church, than piety which seems to wing its flight into more transcendental regions. And, conversely, there are those to whom the chief aspect of Christianity will always be that of Privilege, and whose view of Religion is almost exhausted by one glorious, precious, invaluable word, "Grace." The human model of their piety is the great Apostle of the Gentiles; and in the discipline of their own character, they will do well to keep him before them, and to be followers of him, as he also was of Christ. His form of piety is quite essential to the vitality, energy, and well-being of the Church; its joyousness, its spirit of progress and liberty, its triumph in Evangelical privileges, is as it were a quicker circulation of the lifeblood in the mystical Body of Christ. In a word; let each of us cultivate deeper communion with God through our risen Head according to the particular law (whatever it be) which God hath impressed upon our minds. The one thing needful for us all is the formation of Christ's Image in our own souls, the cleaving to God more closely in trust and love, the more implicit acquiescence than hitherto in our Heavenly Father's will. Along whatever line of thought we are naturally drawn to seek this end, that is the line of thought for us to pursue; we are sure to find many hearts converging to the same great Centre, though it may be along other lines. Towards all such hearts let us be drawn with a true and large Catholic sympathy. We are really looking in the same direction and at the same Object, however widely our points of view may differ. Each of us by himself would be a very imperfect exponent of the mind of the great Master. All together, we may represent Him somewhat more perfectly. Let each see to it that he holds fast the Head by trust and love and adoration. And then all of us together shall come, in the unity of the faith and of the knowledge of the Son of God, unto a perfect man, unto the measure of the stature of the fulness of Christ.

SERMON VI.

JACOB IN LIFE AND IN DEATH.

BY

THE REV. J. W. BURGON, M.A.

FELLOW OF ORIEL COLLEGE, AND VICAR OF S. MARY-THE-VIRGIN'S, OXFORD.

SERMON VI.

Ps. xlvi. 4.

Blessed is he that hath the God of Jacob for his help!

I am much mistaken if we are not better acquainted with Jacob than with any other of the Saints of old. This is not only because he comes before us so largely in his private and domestic relation, but because the character which there comes to view is so intensely human. Hear him interpreting the sign of his bereavement:—"It is my son's coat; an evil beast hath devoured him; Joseph is without doubt torn in pieces." Whereupon he "rends his clothes, and puts sackcloth upon his loins, and mourns for his son many days; and refuses to be comforted:" and says—"For I will go down into the grave unto my son, mourning."—Call to mind that fresh and graceful record of the seven years he served for Rachel, which "seemed to him a few days, for the love he had to her."—Or again, his decision concerning Benjamin: "My son shall *not* go down with you: for his brother is dead, and he is left alone: if mischief befall *him*, then shall ye bring down my grey hairs with sorrow to the grave."[1] His affections are ever strong; his sorrow ever excessive; his anticipation of coming evil ever keen; his recollection of past mercies, ever most deep and tender. How does he linger over any sad passage in his own past history! As with reference to the death of Rachel:—"And as for me, when I came from Padan, Rachel died by me in the land of Canaan, in the way, when yet there was but a little way to come unto Ephrath: and I buried her there, in the way to Ephrath."[2]... How does he enlarge on any circumstance of blessedness; as when he exclaimed at the sight of Joseph,—"Now let me die, since I have seen thy face, because thou art yet alive." And again, before blessing Joseph's two sons,—"I had not thought to see thy face; and lo, GOD hath even shewed me thy seed!"[3] Jacob is intensely *human*, if one may so speak. All his sayings seem to proceed from the same depth of human feeling; and are characterized by the same intensity of human emotion. There is no mistaking

[1] Gen. xxxvii. 23, 34, 35: xxix. 20: xlii. 38.
[2] Gen. xlviii. 7.
[3] Gen. xlvi. 30: xlviii. 11.

the speaker. And this vivid conception of the man, no one recorded circumstance in his history disturbs. We contemplate him with intense interest: we discourse about him with no common confidence.

But the chief thing which gives vividness to the portrait of Jacob is the presence of that brother who from the very first, stands in marked contrast with him. "The boys grew," (says the sacred record:) "and Esau was a cunning hunter, a man of the field: and Jacob was a plain man dwelling in tents." It follows: "And Isaac loved Esau because he did eat of his venison: but Rebecca loved Jacob."[1]

Few words! but they proceed from a mighty Master. Here is the chronicle of forty years of human life. On Esau's side, it is a period of wild adventure and of high animal enjoyment. A jovial hunter,—a careless, easy companion,—the slave of fiery passions,—the creature of quick and generous impulse,—will he not have grown into favour with the inhabitants of the land of his sojourn, into contact with whom his own restless habits must have infallibly brought him? Yes, he will have learnt their ways, acquired their habits, attached himself at last to what he beheld of attractive among them. He was quite a man of the world, in his peculiar oriental

[1] Gen. xxv. 27, 28.

way: kind, warm-hearted, easy, affectionate, and I make no doubt, of most popular manners: not hampered with strong opinions: quite indifferent to dogma. Returning to the tents at Beersheba, after prolonged absence, it is not obscurely hinted that Esau could be even womanly in his attentions towards his aged father; careful to gratify him in a small matter, and in a way which seems to belong rather to the tenderness of the other sex....The very utmost that can be said for Esau, has now been said.

As for Jacob, it must be freely admitted that the epithet applied to his brother seems rather to belong of right to *him:* while one fails to perceive his title to the description of being "a plain man," (*ἄνθρωπος ἄπλαστος*). But the explanation is obvious. "A cunning hunter" is the fitting praise of one who excels in the sports of the field: while Jacob's guilelessness,—(for *that* is doubtless the meaning of the word,)—refers, not to the method by which the man endeavoured to accomplish his purposes and attain his end; but to his single-heartedness in GOD'S sight; the sincerity of his love towards GOD; the plain downright childlike faith with which he clung to GOD'S promises, and the guileless earnestness with which he coveted the Blessing which had been his sire's, and his sire's sire's before him.

We must attend to this feature in Jacob's character: else we shall fail to judge rightly of the rest of the story. And, standing before some to whom the picture which we just have drawn of Esau's habits will effectually recommend itself,—(as, apart from its less obvious, *fatal* adjuncts, it reasonably may,)—I feel bound to invite your attention, further, to what seems to be implied by the declaration that Jacob was "a dweller in tents." We must recollect the relation in which the chosen line stood towards Canaan,—the land of their sojourn. They were to be its future lords: and were only not put into immediate possession, because, (as the righteous Judge Himself declared,) "the iniquity of the Amorites was not yet full."[1] All around them therefore dwelt an idolatrous and an accursed race, with which they were clearly to have the least possible intercourse. They were, on the contrary, to cherish their own pure and precious traditions, looking beyond the present into a glorious future; and through the vista of Canaan, (which, in the fourth generation was to belong to Abraham's seed,) fasten their gaze upon the Land of everlasting Life.

Such had been the course of Abraham: such was the course of Isaac. They confessed themselves to

[1] Gen. xv. 16.

be but strangers and pilgrims:[1] and lived like men who seek a country. O yes! "They are not to be heard which feign that the old Fathers did look only for transitory promises." It was faith in CHRIST'S most precious Blood which sustained them; and they saw,—afar off, indeed, and dimly; yet they *saw*,—"the Day of CHRIST, and were glad:" they beheld the sacrifice of His Death, and the Redemption and recovery of our fallen race, which was to follow; and they looked for the City which hath the twelve glorious foundations, whose maker and builder is GOD! They had their daily, and their weekly rite, be sure; and the priestly office was fully recognized among them; and they had their complex curious Ritual, like the Church of a later day. And we may be persuaded that the cunning hunter who trod in the steps of Nimrod and of Ishmael, made light of, while he turned his back upon, the ancestral worship of the line of Shem:—just as we may be convinced that the same service of the Most High was the joy and crown of him whose posterity afterwards called their dwelling-places "*the tents of Jacob.*" Nor may we think of Jacob as dwelling solitary, because he will have been a feeder of sheep, and because he dwelt at home. For upwards of a hundred years, Noah,

[1] Heb. xi. 13.

Shem, Arphaxad, Salah, Eber, Peleg, Reu, Serug, Nahor, and Terah, were all alive together:—such a College of Saints as the world had never beheld before, and will never behold again; and although all these were now dead, yet with their descendants must have survived a school of sacred learning, in which Jacob may well have become a great proficient. For nineteen years he will have held direct intercourse with Eber,—who for upwards of two hundred and fifty years had dwelt with Noah. Isaac himself was able to transmit to Jacob the traditional lore which for fifty long years he had derived from the very lips of Shem,—a man who had known the World before the Flood. Is it possible to recollect all this, and not to behold in the statement that Jacob,—(single-hearted and guileless towards GOD,)—eschewed the roving life of Esau,—Can we, I ask, overlook in this, the implied revelation of days spent in holy thought, and in earnest prayer?...Add to it all the solemn circumstance that a prophecy had been delivered to his Mother from the very mouth of GOD, that "the elder should serve the younger;" and there is no room for surprise at the disclosure made in Holy Writ concerning the Mother's abiding partiality for her younger son. A voice from the ancient Patriarchal hearth of Beersheba declares that "Isaac loved

Esau, because he did eat of his venison: but," (it is added,)—"*Rebekah loved Jacob!*"

The Divine Oracle which she had received when "she went to inquire of the LORD," must ever occupy a prominent place in our meditations on the character of Jacob. The Mother "*went* to inquire;" (meaning that she repaired to that holy place where GOD was wont to communicate with men,—as afterwards in the Tabernacle, and later in the Temple); and she received for answer, that she bore within herself two nations, and should give birth to two manner of people: "and the one people shall be stronger than the other people; and the elder shall serve the younger."[1] The voice of GOD had long before limited MESSIAH to the descendants of Abraham: the finger of GOD now pointed out Jacob,—albeit the younger son,—as the destined inheritor of the blessing. Such was the secret over which his Mother brooded with all a Mother's earnestness: the secret which she will have instilled into his youthful mind, teaching him to regard it as the main object of his desire. How GOD would ever give accomplishment to the word He had spoken, Jacob saw not; for the Birthright was another's. At last, on a day, Esau comes in from the field faint from hunting. "There was a

[1] Gen. xx. 23.

famine in the land."[1] Jacob had prepared for himself pottage. "And Esau said to Jacob, Feed me, I pray thee, with that red red,"—(the evidence of his impatience surviving to this hour on the imperishable page; and the colour of the pottage which moved his appetite so strongly, being for ever reflected in his very name:)—"feed me, for I am faint." —"Sell me this day thy birthright," replied the other: the secret longing of his soul rising up instantly to his lips, and finding spontaneous expression...."And Esau said, Behold, I am at the point to die:" (surely he magnified his need!) "and what profit shall this birthright do to me?" (surely therein he despised his birthright!)..."Swear to me this day," was the impatient rejoinder. "And Esau sware unto him: and he sold his birthright unto Jacob. Then Jacob gave Esau bread and pottage of lentiles; and he did eat and drink, and rose up, and went his way:"[2]—the way of the profane man and the fornicator![3]

My brethren,—There is a moment in the life of most men, a turning point, which is decisive of the history and the character. No one knows what the act may be which is fraught with such tremendous

[1] Gen. xxvi. 1. [2] Gen. xxv. 29—34.
[3] Heb. xii. 16.

consequences. It may be a very contemptible act,—vile as the coveting "a morsel of meat;" and yet it may be fatal and final. From that moment, the character declines, and the path is downward; and the remote consequences of the act,—what eye shall presume to foresee? It may be irregular, scarcely perceptible progress, like the darkening of the days in winter: but it is certain. Thus was it in the case before us. Behold those two brothers in the tent, and witness the insignificant transaction to all appearance in which they are engaged. We know what it led to, in their own persons. The feud between Esau and Jacob was never healed; not even when long years had rolled by,—for the children of Israel, Jacob's descendants, on their return from Egypt, were threatened with the sword if they dared to pass through Edom's border.[1] At the Babylonish captivity, Edom stood by rejoicing.[2] The two races were for ever at enmity. Behold, at last, Herod the Idumean, (that is, the Edomite,) confronting Jacob's great descendant, our Incarnate LORD, and aggravating the bitterness of His Cross and Passion!...See to what a height of sin the gratification of one lust had led! Shall it not make us tremble for ourselves, lest *we* should ever fall under the like condemnation with Esau?

[1] Numb. xx. 14—21. [2] Ps. cxxxvii. 7. Obad. v. 10—14.

Meanwhile, the secret is kept close. The Blessing has not yet been bestowed, though the Birthright has been parted with: and, mark you, Jacob is contented to wait on, for forty-five years without it. At last, when Isaac has attained the age at which his brother Ishmael died,[1]—sick and anticipating his own end, Isaac proposes to make a formal conveyance to Esau of the Blessing which had descended through Abraham, from GOD. We all remember the circumstances of dignity with which that patriarchal act was invested. The eldest son, clad in his perfumed priestly robes, having given his Father food, together with Bread and Wine, knelt down to receive by imposition of hands, the prevailing Benediction. We all remember too the eagerness with which the partial Mother contrives how Jacob shall supplant Esau. This last has gone to the field in all the self-confidence which characterizes sin. He makes no confession of his past act. He thinks he shall speed in his hunting, and flatters himself with the prospect of speedily enjoying the Blessing, although he is well aware that he has long since forfeited his right to it. Meantime, the robes are put on Jacob,—not by any means reluctant, yet terror-stricken at what he is di-

[1] Viz. 137 years,—which was also the age of Levi, of Amram, and of Abraham at the time of Sarah's death.

rected by his Mother to do. The singular details of the deception, no heart can ever forget; and the circumstantial untruth which Jacob told, when questioned by his perplexed parent; as well as the undoubting, hearty, glorious benediction which followed. Taking occasion from the fragrance of the myrrh, aloes, and cassia in which the goodly raiment had been laid up,[1]—"See," (cried the Patriarch,) "the smell of my son is as the smell of a field which the LORD hath blessed. Therefore, GOD give thee of the dew of Heaven, and the fatness of the Earth, and plenty of corn and wine. Let people serve thee, and nations bow down to thee. Be lord over thy brethren, and let thy mother's sons bow down to thee. Cursed be every one that curseth thee, and blessed be he that blesseth thee."[2]

I am not concerned to defend Jacob's share in this transaction. It *cannot* be right to tell an untruth. It *must* be wrong for a son to deceive his Father. But I very boldly assert *this*, that GOD'S Saints of old time do not come before us in the Bible for *our* judicial sentence. Those whom GOD approves, are there for our admiration: those whom GOD rejects,

[1] Compare the following places:—Ex. xxx. 23, 24, 30. Lev. viii. 30. Ps. xlv. 8.

[2] Gen. xxvii. 27—9.

are there for us also to condemn. Now, the fact that Jacob, a fugitive from his Father's house, is straightway blessed with a vision of Angels,—and with the assurance of GOD'S favour and protection,—("Behold, I am with thee, and will keep thee in all places whither thou goest, and will bring thee again into this land: for I will not leave thee until I have done that which I have spoken to thee of"[1]):—this, I say, *proves* that Jacob's character was of the kind which GOD likes: while the subsequent rejection of Esau as clearly establishes the fact that *he* was in GOD'S sight hateful. Twenty long years are spent in Padan Aram, and the Divine promise is renewed:—"Return unto the land of thy fathers and of thy kindred, and I will be with thee."[2] And on Jacob's return, two bright companies of GOD'S Host,—two glittering bands of Angel warriors, again meet him.[3] From *this* point you must reason backwards, if you would form a true estimate of Jacob. You will perhaps see some extenuation of his conduct in the fact that he had acted in obedience to his Mother's repeated and earnest commands: ("Upon me be thy curse, my son, only obey my voice!") You will consider the stimulus supplied by the famous prophecy which had gone before. You will note the low esteem in which Esau held his

[1] Gen. xxviii. 15. [2] Gen. xxxi. 3. [3] Gen. xxxii. 12.

Birthright; and consider that when it had once become Jacob's, Esau had no longer any title to the Blessing. Further, you will note that Jacob and Rebekah too were severely punished for their undoubted fault. He, a forlorn exile, whom the drought consumed by day and the frost by night, duped and ill-treated by Laban, for twenty long years; afterwards, punished severely in his children; constrained at last to exclaim that "the days of the years of his pilgrimage had been few and evil:"[1]—Jacob, I say, from first to last felt the chastening Hand of GOD. As for the fond Mother, she, instead of the "few days" of absence which she contemplated, was destined never to behold the face of that beloved son again. She lived, she died, weary of her life because of the idolatrous daughters of Heth, whom Esau had married.[2] On behalf of both Mother and son, we shall be careful to remember that *Truth* is emphatically a Gospel Grace: that the men of that age walked by a feebler light, and set before themselves a less lofty standard, than was afterwards proposed to a redeemed race: that "Grace and Truth came by JESUS CHRIST:" that "*the Spirit of Truth*" had not as yet been given.[3]

[1] Gen. xxxi. 40, 41: xlvii. 9. [2] Gen. xxvii. 44, 46.
[3] S. John i. 17: xvi. 13.

But the main thing remains yet unspoken. The clue to the Divine favour which attended Jacob, is to be found in his earnest piety,—his unmistakable zeal for GOD'S honour and glory;—his burning faith in GOD'S promises, and his passionate desire to inherit them. The secret of his blessedness lay in *this*, that he had from the first given his heart unreservedly to GOD. Nothing knew *he*, of that vile indifferentism which is the plague-spot of these last days. Nothing knew he of the fashionable lukewarmness in the things of GOD. Witness his mysterious struggle at Jabbok with the Angel: and that bold rejoinder of his, when the other said, "Let me go, for the day breaketh:"—witness, I say, his determined answer,—"I will not let thee go except thou bless me!"[1] He was a profoundly religious character;—the fear and the love of GOD, and an habitual sense of dependence on *Him* for protection, as well as a constant reference of every blessing, every trial to *Him*,—finding constant expression in Jacob's life and conduct. Take his very striving for the Birthright,—his patient waiting for the Blessing: and consider its real nature. Does any one suppose it was at all akin to the lust of wealth and power which might be inferred from a similar act in these days? GOD forbid! Full well Jacob knew

[1] Gen. xxxii. 26.

that the Blessing which he coveted was spiritual, and the inheritance which GOD had promised to his Father, was heavenly. *GOD* therefore was the thing that he longed for throughout. He walked as seeing Him who is invisible; and did not consider that GOD'S promise had failed, though for twenty long years he was an afflicted exile: for thirty-three years more a sorrowful pilgrim: though he bowed down before his brother, calling him 'Lord;' and though he finally ended his days in Egypt, far from the Land of Promise and the grave of his fathers.... The whole man comes out strikingly in his prayer to GOD in a moment of deepest anxiety and alarm:—"O GOD of my Father Abraham, and GOD of my Father Isaac;—the LORD which saidst unto me, Return unto thy country, and to thy kindred, and I will deal well with thee:—I am not worthy of the least of all the mercies, and of all the truth which thou hast showed unto thy servant; for with my staff I passed over this Jordan, and now I am become two bands. Deliver me, I pray thee, from the hand of my brother, from the hand of Esau; for I fear him: lest he will come and smite me, and the Mother with the children. And Thou saidst,—I will surely do thee good, and make thy seed as the sand of the sea, which cannot be numbered for multitude."[1]... Or again, call to mind any of Jacob's casual sayings, and the piety of his diposition comes unmistakably to view. When, for instance, Esau met him on his return from Paran, and asked,—"Who are those with thee?" "The Children *which* GOD *hath graciously given* thy servant,"—replied the other. Presently, Esau inquires the meaning of the droves he had met; and on learning that they were intended as a present,—"*I have enough, my brother,*" (he said): "*Keep that thou hast unto thyself.*" To which, Jacob makes answer,—"Take, I pray thee, my blessing that is brought to thee: *because* GOD *hath dealt graciously with me.*"... Even when he blesses the two sons of Joseph, it is not without a gush of grateful recollection for past mercies:—"GOD, before whom my fathers Abraham and Isaac did walk,—the GOD which fed me all my life long unto this day: the Angel which redeemed me from all evil,—bless the lads!"... Nay, behold the dying Saint mapping out prophetically the Land of Canaan among the heads of the future tribes who stood about his bed; and notice how, after the blessing of his seventh son, he pauses to exclaim,—as if gathering up the spirit of his whole life into a single strong cry,—"I have waited for Thy Salvation, O LORD!"

[1] Gen. xxxii. 9—12.

Such then was the disposition which GOD disciplined,—the heart which, throughout the days of the years of its pilgrimage, GOD fashioned by suffering, until it was prepared to enter into glory..... "Blessed is he that hath the GOD of Jacob for *his* help!"

For we are not to suppose, for an instant, that the outline of Jacob's actual life corresponded with the pattern or image in the Divine mind. Full, in the sight of GOD, must ever be, not only what we are, but also what we might have been, had we made a different use of our opportunities; availed ourselves to better purpose of His checks and His warnings, and the guidance of His good Spirit. We behold in the eventful life of Jacob, a Hand more than human, over-ruling and controlling,—yet not interfering nor constraining. Those mighty Fingers move in the outer circle of causation,—a region far above, out of our sight. We give it the name of 'Providence;' but it is in truth a region without a name, pervaded only by GOD'S inscrutable Will. And there, the eagerness for the Birth-right, — because it sprung from a pure and lofty motive,—was suffered to result in fruition: and yet, because the Blessing was not obtained without a large admixture of the dross of sin, the man was made to go heavily all the days of the years of his life. He had deliberately made choice of GOD'S Service; and so, GOD was not ashamed to be called *his* GOD. And yet, for his craft towards his aged and dim-sighted Sire, he was punished with craft from Laban, and in his age with treacherous impiety from his sons. *That* forcible appropriation to himself of the Promises,—(which GOD would doubtless have given him in another, and an innocent way, had he waited the LORD'S leisure,)—met with its own appropriate reward. "A Syrian ready to perish," how did he begin and end his days an exile from the Land which was the type of his heavenly inheritance! Strong, only because he had taken the LORD for his strength:—happy, only in that he waited for the LORD'S salvation!

It is time to make an end.—Second to nothing in Jacob's life, for interest, dignity and wonder, is Jacob's deathbed: wherein the destinies of a people, and the rudiments of Heaven itself, are touchingly mixed up with circumstantial details concerning the things of earth. "I am to be gathered unto my people,"—(such are his last recorded words:) "Bury me with my Fathers in the cave that is in the field of Ephron the Hittite: in the cave that is in the field of Machpelah, which is before Mamre, in the land of Canaan, which Abraham bought with the field of Ephron the Hittite for a possession of a burying-place. There they buried Abraham, and Sarah his wife; there they buried Isaac, and Rebekah his wife; and there I buried Leah. The purchase of the field and of the cave that is therein was from the children of Heth."[1]... Side by side with this, is many a mysterious image of the things which should be hereafter: as the striking anticipation of the Death and Resurrection of CHRIST, shadowed forth by One that "couched as a Lion:" and the inquiry, "Who shall rouse Him up?"—How startlingly minute again is that vision of One "binding His foal unto the Vine, and His ass's colt unto the choice Vine"!—And how solemnly is CHRIST'S Passion shadowed forth in that image of One who "*washed His garments in the blood of grapes*"!.... Doubtless it is somewhat thus that Heaven itself opens to the eyes of GOD'S dying Saints!.... The various dispensations of His Providence,—bruised affections, disappointed desires, constancy exposed to a life-long trial:—these are the instruments which GOD employs for Man's discipline; and finally, for his perfection. Darkened hopes, and withdrawn supports, and, again, spiritual consolations and assurances of GOD'S mercy and favour;—by all such methods He is for ever drawing *us* unto Himself, preparing *us*

[1] Gen. xlix. 29—32.

to become the heirs of Glory.... O thou, whoever hearest me,—try to realise this more in thyself! See GOD more about thine own path: learn to recognise Him more in the events of every passing day: walk more as seeing Him who is invisible: *submit* to be fashioned by *Him* who shapes thy life after the counsel of His perfect Will!

We have a childish way of talking about Heaven as "the place which good men go to,"—and the like,—which carries with it no obscure intimation that we entertain a less than childish,—even a beggarly apprehension of the things of GOD. Hear an Apostle discoursing of Heaven, or rather, of that which alone makes Heaven an object of desire, viz. the Life in Glory. "Lay hold," he says,—"*Lay hold* on Eternal Life." He speaks of it as something which in a real sense, is to be apprehended *now*. "*This* is Life Eternal," (saith our SAVIOUR,) "to know Thee the only true GOD, and JESUS CHRIST whom Thou hast sent."... There is no one image or expression in Scripture which countenances the belief that from a life of carelessness, coldness, hypocrisy,—joined to the show of a fair outward moral life, much less from a life of profaneness, impurity, unbelief, self-indulgence, sloth,—there is any exit into the bowers of Bliss. And the heart of man knows it; and so,

—ever and anon, as the ages of the World roll by,—a hoarse Voice is heard, stipulating that at least the pains of Hell shall not be *for ever.* Death, if you will, (says the Voice:) yes,—the second Death: but not Death eternal! And the pent-up groan of a sinful world murmurs low applause.—So is it in our own day,—so is it at this very hour. O do not ye,—O beware lest *ye,*—by private word or public act, swell that accursed Voice,—a Voice suggested by the Father of lies, who dared say to our first mother, and through *her* to *us,*—"Ye shall *not* surely die."

There is a mystery in unrepented, unforgiven sin, which contradicts the whole nature of GOD: and to suppose that a greater or less amount of mere human suffering can ever expiate it, is to suppose that Eternity can be measured off by Time. Nay, it is to insult the mercies of the Eternal, so to speak; as if He could do at the end of an age what He refuses to do *now.* And what, (let me ask,)—What is to become of Everlasting *Life,* if Everlasting Death is discovered to be a Dream?... But I turn from this whole speculation,—awful and beyond us as it is,—with disgust and abhorrence. The whole tenor of Holy Scripture is against such dreams. Every utterance of the SPIRIT is an invitation to take far higher ground. "*Put ye on* the LORD JESUS CHRIST." "Be ye holy, for I am holy." "Be ye also *perfect.*" "He that believeth in Me, though he were dead, yet shall he live: and whosoever liveth and believeth on Me, shall never die!" "Come unto Me, all that labour and are heavy laden, and I will refresh you."... The life to come must begin *now.* If we would sit down with Abraham, Isaac, and Jacob, in the Kingdom of CHRIST, we must, on Earth, make Him our GOD, who is not ashamed to be called theirs. We must walk as Jacob walked: submissive to the same Heavenly discipline; and in constant dependence on the same Heavenly will; and in hearty Faith, as partakers in the same promises, and heirs with him of the same Heavenly inheritance. "Blessed," of a truth, in that hour when flesh and heart faileth,—"Blessed is he that hath the GOD of Jacob for his help!"

SERMON VII.

GOD THE HOPE AND JOY OF THE PENITENT.

BY

THE REV. T. T. CARTER, M.A.

RECTOR OF CLEWER, BERKSHIRE.

SERMON VII.

ST LUKE VII. 48—50.

And He said unto her, Thy sins are forgiven. And they that sat at meat with Him began to say within themselves, Who is this that forgiveth sins also? And He said unto the woman, Thy faith hath saved thee; go in peace.

THESE words close the history of that deeply touching scene at the house of Simon the Pharisee, where Jesus sat as a guest, when the sinful woman from the city came in with the alabaster box of ointment, and anointed His feet. My object is not to dwell on the details of the history, but rather to point out the remarkable contrast of thought and feeling manifested towards the Penitent by the different persons present. The persons are, Simon the Pharisee, the company assembled at his house, our Lord, and the special object of their common interest, the penitent woman. She had entered the guest-chamber under a strong impulse, pursued with the agony of her remorse, and laying hold with intense eagerness on the hope of peace that had dawned upon her, lavish in her love, stooping to any abasement which her public self-condemnation might incur, anxious to make the costliest sacrifice, if only relief could be obtained for the sore anguish lying at her heart. Hence the pouring the precious ointment on our Lord, the continuing to wash His feet with tears, and kiss them, and wipe them with her hair.

Though a striking instance, she was but one among many of the multitudes of true penitents, whom the grace of God has drawn to Himself, their souls absorbed in the one intense craving for mercy. The point to be observed regarding her, is the manner in which she was received, the thoughts expressed at the sight of her, and our Lord's conduct towards her. As the poor sinner passed under Simon's eye, a cold disregard and silent neglect was visible in his countenance. He presided at the feast with the same zest, talked as blithely on its passing topics, and preserved the same exclusive attention to the decorum of his state and position, equally as though this penitent woman had never emerged from her haunts of sin, and startled the festive company with her wild enthusiasm of despair and love. It was precisely the same to Simon the Pharisee, whether she continued to ply her impure trade in the purlieus of the city, sinking daily more and more deeply into the hopeless misery which such a life involves, or whether she made the immense effort which it must have cost to break away from the bondage which had once enthralled her, and, in spite of the ridicule and reckless scorn of her companions, rush wildly forth into the face of day, into the light of purity, to implore peace and restoration of life,—the same to him, undisturbed and imperturbable in the pride of his caste, and in the cold narrowness of his conventional self-righteousness. Simon is the type of all true Pharisees, and his judgement in this case represents the opinions of no insignificant portion of society sharing a like traditionary creed.

The assembled company were looking on with amazement at the conduct of our Lord towards the penitent woman. His allowing her to approach so near to Him, to touch Him, to kiss His feet; to remain clinging to Him; His look, His words of tenderness, not merely His absolving her, but all that had passed before, startled them; for when they say within themselves, "Who is this that forgiveth sins *also?*"—the absolution was evidently an additional, not the sole, cause of their wonder. Strange, that He should so demean Himself, so notice her, so allow her familiarities, her appeals of love, so meet her with kindness and encouragement; but stranger far, the very height of perplexity, that He should "forgive her sins." These persons could not see the meaning of the love that wins souls, nor recognise its effect upon the heart of the sinner. They distrusted efforts to reclaim the outcast. They feared degradation from intercourse with the degraded. Moreover their eyes were blinded, so that they could not discern God there present. In that Voice which at the very moment was shedding peace within the soul of the penitent woman, and re-creating her unto newness of life, they had not ears to hear more than the voice of man. Nor could they see the possibility of sin being entirely put away on earth. Only they shewed a wondering mind, questioning, who He was who assumed such authority. These men were the exponents of the feelings of a great mass of society, before whom miracles of redeeming love are being continually wrought, but are dimly, if at all, apprehended.

Amidst these manifestations of human scorn and blindness sat calmly the mysterious stranger Guest, Who had attracted to Himself the whole attention, and wondering gaze of the company. He was there revealing the thoughts which, contrary to the thoughts of men, prevail in Heaven towards the Penitent, and which He had come on earth in the very substance of man's own nature, and in man's own voice, to manifest to the world.

Twice in the history of mankind God has personally and openly revealed Himself on earth, to shew what otherwise could never have been imagined, what no mere words of revelation would ever have availed to depict, the feelings of the Heart of God towards the Penitent. Once in the beginning, after the first acts of sin, He appeared for this purpose. What a soothing relief it must have been to the terrified consciences of the first transgressors, that not a mere voice of hope, instinctively springing within their own souls, was stirred, not merely a prophet's voice spoke, nor even an angel, nor an archangel, but God Himself, the Almighty, appeared and spoke and reasoned and pleaded with the sinner; and Himself, as the sinner turned to Him, sealed the hope of his forgiveness. What to Adam and Cain must have been the revival of hope, the sense of consolation in the assurances thus given, first to Adam, "Thou, thy seed, shalt bruise the serpent's head[1];" and afterwards to Cain, "If thou doest not well, sin," *i. e.* the sin-offering, "lieth at the door[2]."

[1] Gen. iii. 15. [2] Gen. iv. 7.

These, the earliest, the primeval manifestations of God, were intended to leave, and surely must have left, a profound impression on the minds of the faithful during all the earlier ages, enabling them to look beyond this visible world, to see through it, to see the mind of God, to hear the voice of God, to understand what hope of reconciliation awaited the Penitent in His Presence. When afterwards, according to the merciful provisions of the Mosaic covenant, the Israelite stood at the door of the Temple with his victim to be offered, his hands on its head confessing his sins, and acknowledging his own desert of death, but pleading the promise of acceptance through the death of the victim offered in his stead, —he could look through the veil of these outward ordinances, and beyond the ministering Priesthood, and see by faith the very Presence of God, as He appeared to his forefathers, and in this vision discern his true ground of hope. The manifestation of God Himself formed the background of the mysterious ministrations of mercy, which his outward eye beheld. Behind the screen of the visible service, in which men alone were seen employed, the God of his fathers still appeared to the Penitent, as the one sure stay of hope, and source of joy, thus freshly awakened in his soul as he there sought for restored life. The voices of the prophets continued to perpetuate the meaning of the priestly service of the Temple, and kept before the Penitent's mind the truth of the assurance which their old traditions taught. Similar words to these of Isaiah echoed through all the prophetical utterances; "I, even I," (the living God, the personal Jehovah, speaking through the prophet,) "am He that blotteth out thy transgressions for Mine own sake, and will not remember thy sins[1]."

The second time that God appeared for this purpose was in His Incarnation, the manifestation of God in the flesh, when the same truth was revealed again, only now with wondrously increased fulness, and in unspeakably more touching forms.

There were manifestly two main influences at work in that great moving of the souls of men, which heaved to and fro, like the waters of the great deep, around Jesus Christ. The great gatherings, such, *e.g.*, as that of the many thousands who thronged after Him into the wilderness listening to His words, whom He fed, who would have made Him a King, who afterwards passed round to the other side of the lake to anticipate His coming, when He had hidden Himself from them; these were the representatives of a profound stirring of hearts throughout the whole land. Men were roused by the new teaching, by the

[1] Isai. xliii. 25.

appeal to a higher sense of humanity, by the beauty, the holiness, the love, the greatness, the authority, such as never before had been seen in human form, a manifestation so unearthly, and yet so true to the instinctive cravings of man's nature. They were won by the hopes which were held out to them of the new kingdom, and the higher destiny opening before mankind in the "regeneration, when the Son of Man shall sit upon the throne of His glory[1]."

It was a public movement involving a great revolution of thought and hope in the minds of the people; even "the common people heard Him gladly[2]."

But there was a more secret and inner movement stirred, in a smaller circle indeed, but one of yet profounder sensations, and far more powerful energies, among those who were "weary and heavy laden" with the burden of life, and hopelessly sinking under the overwhelming consciousness of sin. Such *e.g.* was the man, out of whom the legion of devils was cast; and again the blind man, who was charged to take heed, lest "a worse thing come upon" him; and Mary Magdalene, who, rescued from the grasp of Satan, gave herself and her substance to minister to the glory of her Deliverer.

[1] S. Matt. xix. 28. [2] S. Mark xii. 37.

Our Lord had laid His spell on these sufferers, who were drawn by a power now for the first time acting on their hearts, and which they felt to be full of a rest and hope unknown before.

It has fallen to my lot to speak of God, and especially God in Christ, as the hope and joy of the Penitent. It is in the workings of His grace on this inner circle of disciples, that the truth which I have undertaken to uphold, is specially brought out to view. There is through His grace a communion of God with the soul on which this restored life depends; and in the secret revelations of His Spirit a new world of thought and feeling opens before the mind of the Penitent, leading him to a true and stedfast peace. Let us consider some of the saving influences which are thus operating as the true grounds of hope and joy.

1. God alone can impress upon the soul a full sense of its sinfulness. The true consciousness of sinfulness arises only from a knowledge of the true standard from which the soul has fallen. It is the sight—the consciousness of the purer, holier life, that draws out the sense of degradation, and inward loathing. This consciousness arises, as the perception grows of a higher standard of humanity, and of God's

rightful claims on human life. It must therefore depend on the measure of true life set before the soul; the truer the perception of holiness, the deeper the consciousness of sin. But the true standard of man's holiness, and so the true measure of man's guilt, cannot be known except through Christ. Contrast the character of the repentance, which was stirred even around S. John the Baptist. The people thronged to hear him, confessing their sins. But what was the standard of life, which it was then possible to set before them? "He that hath two coats, let him impart to him that hath none; and he that hath meat, let him do likewise." "Then came also publicans to be baptized, and said unto him, Master, what shall we do? And he said unto them, Exact no more than that which is appointed you. And the soldiers likewise demanded of Him, saying, And what shall we do? And he said unto them, Do violence to no man, neither accuse any falsely; and be content with your wages[1]."

Such was the standard of human life, which at that time the Prophet could put before men. And it did stir penitent souls to ask of him guidance in the way of peace. But what a far higher standard arose before men's minds, when Jesus lived and spoke!

[1] S. Luke iii. 11—14.

It was the bringing a new light into the darkness, awakening a new world of the most powerful convictions, before which the conscience arose with a self-condemnation that could not rest, till it had poured itself forth in confession, in tears, in cries for mercy at the feet of Jesus. Now the very foundations of a saving repentance rest on this true perception of the sin, which burdens and endangers the soul's life. Nor can the Penitent venture to trust, that life or joy can ever be restored, if still left in darkness as to his real danger.

2. Again, our Lord satisfied that longing for the true searching of its real state, which lies deep in a sincere penitent's soul. A true penitent does not desire palliations of his offences, the ascribing his sins, *e.g.*, to unfortunate circumstances, or to excusable infirmity, or mere natural temperament, or the ardour of youth; or the attempt to justify them by the usages and allowances of society. Such treatment only throws back the Penitent upon himself, leaving him still unsatisfied and desponding. The unrest is caused by the soul's longing for truth, even to its own greater condemnation. 'Tell me all the depth of my fall. Hide nothing from me, hide me not from myself, now that the conviction that I am fallen, has broken in upon me. Let me

know the worst.' It is the desire that the cleansing of conscience which has cost so much should be done thoroughly. There is a feeling in the case of bodily illness, that the only relief or cure lies in the eradication of the whole diseased part. A similar instinct is aroused in the consciousness of the soul's sickness; it cannot rest until it feels, that the full light has shined into every part, and left no secret sore untouched. Closely connected moreover with this feeling is the longing felt by the Penitent not to appear in false colours, to appear true at least before One Who can know him truly, before Whom nothing can be hid; that at least in one eye he may feel himself real and honest. To be able to say, 'There is One Who knows me as I truly am,' is to a true penitent unspeakable rest. This relief is felt in confession to a fellow-creature. He has made another partner of the secret which is burdening his soul. He does not walk altogether as a hypocrite among men, if but one knows the hidden truth. But the knowledge of the full extent of the fall, of the full truth of the sinner's sinful state, can be revealed only to God, Who searcheth the heart. The full rest therefore of being seen and known in the full and simple reality of one's actual state, is possible only as one stands thus exposed before God.

3. Again, it is God, and He alone, who can give the hope of restoration. And it is this which lies beneath the deep craving, such as stirred the penitent who clung to our Saviour's feet. There is in the Penitent's soul the instinctive conviction, that peace can be had only in the soul's renewal. The mere sense of forgiveness without a change, or the idea of a change, without a trust that the change may be adequate to the soul's conception, cannot satisfy. To become pure is the craving of one who groans over his impurity, not merely to be forgiven his repeated acts of sin. To acquire the power of self-denial is the longing of the intemperate, not merely to obtain repeated absolution for repeated falls. To have the simplicity of truth, and the courage to be open, is the aspiration of one who stands overwhelmed with shame at repeated falsehood, not merely a trust that the past may be forgotten. To be able to love God, not merely to mourn over His coldness, though this too is a great gift of God; to be able to pray fervently and stedfastly, not merely to sorrow at feebleness and continual wanderings; to become transformed into a reverent, devout, recollected spirit, not merely to recall with shame the irreverence and profanations of past heedless days,—such conversions manifestly are alone able to satisfy the Pe-

nitent's awakened earnestness. But it is in God alone that such restoration can be found. Such renewing grace was found in contact with the holiness of Christ. It had a power of imparting itself. It opened within the soul of the penitent a consciousness of the infinite possibilities of the life of renewed humanity. Consider the case of Zacchæus. He was, if like other publicans, a hard man. He was habituated to dishonourable gains, to disregard the laws of benevolence, and devoid of pity for the poor. But the approach of Christ to his house and to himself opened a new world of thought, and caused a complete revolution of ideas. It struck the spark of fire within him, and kindled in him higher, nobler views of life; and in the change that passed within his soul new energies of self-sacrifice and love awoke. A sense of newly-found joy animated the words in which he expressed his resolve to dedicate his substance to the glory of God, and the good of his fellow-creatures. "Behold, Lord, the half of my goods I give to the poor; and if I have taken any thing from any man by false accusation, I restore him fourfold[1]."

4. Again, God, and God alone, can make a perfectly fair allowance for the weaknesses which induced

[1] S. Luke xix. 8.

the hated sin, and the strength of the temptations which drew out the fatal tendencies. Though there is in the soul of the Penitent a desire to be judged with strictness and even severity, there is a longing also for equity, a deep and true consciousness that to acknowledge what good there may yet be lingering within, or to allow for one's difficulties and the strength of adverse circumstances, is due to our nature's highest instincts. There is a large noble way of regarding sin, and there is a narrow view of it. A different aspect of sin presents itself to one who has experienced and calmly estimated its power at work within himself under the influence of exciting causes, and who knows the weakness and possible self-deceit of the human heart; or on the other hand, to one who judges by mere sentiment, or with a fictitious scrupulousness, or a supposed righteous austerity; or worse still, in ignorance of his own heart.

The purer the man who has stood the test of long struggling with sin, the more large and free and considerate will be his judgments, the more able to enter into, and allow for, all that may be truly set against another's guilt, or pleaded in its palliation. To look calmly at the sin, to weigh its hatefulness, not so much with the thought to condemn, but to heal, as a thing which, alas! is common to man, and must be met and mastered by patient, tender, forgiving gentleness—this is to be in harmony with the mind of Christ. How surely does such a spirit mark His dealing with all who penitently approached Him. How calmly, how unupbraidingly, with what simplicity, with what readiness to forget, to bury the past, with what quick eagerness to save rather than to repel; to raise and console and assure, rather than lay the lightest weight of discouragement which might tend to break the bruised reed!

5. Again, God and He alone can give a perfect sympathy. A peculiar sense of loneliness besets the penitent who has deeply sinned. There is in him the feeling that none can be so bad as himself, that if only others knew what he was, they would shun him; that because of his greater sinfulness none can ever understand what he feels, or imagine half the evil that continually is at work within him. Even kindness is thought to be unreal, and with reluctance accepted, because it is thought to be given only on an untrue supposition; and sympathy thus offered appears to be merely external, neither are the secret springs of the soul touched by it.

But there can be no such drawbacks in the perfect sympathy of Christ. He has penetrated the depths of human iniquity, felt all its weight, and suffered from its malice, and yet with all this knowledge, and after all these sufferings, loved the sinful race so well, as to become for its sake "obedient unto death, even the death of the cross." He must surely feel for us and with us, if He could so stoop and so endure to suffer for us. We cannot doubt, that as He permitted the woman from the city to cling to Him in the presence of that company, while He knew the sin which was in her soul, and all her past history, and her "sins were many;" so He will receive, and pity, and give His Heart's deep interest and care for every one alike who thus humbly draws near, and seeks, as she sought, His love and saving, healing virtue. Nothing was hidden from Him, and yet He drew her to Him, and blessed her before the upbraiding world, bearing witness to the truth of her love.

6. Once more, and I have reserved as the last instance of rest in God for the Penitent, what in truth would more fitly have been mentioned first, because it is the groundwork of all other influences which may work in him true hope and joy. It is God alone Who can cleanse the guilt of sin away. In the dark maddening hours, during which there rise before the sinner's soul the terrors of the last judgment, and the frightful endless torments of the infinite

abyss, and the wailings of the lost, and the cries of irremediable despair, and the terrible phantoms of devils in chains under darkness in their prison-house, all rays of light which issue from the Presence of God are excluded for evermore. When such thoughts come over the soul, as in the night visions, or under depressed health, or spirits, or in subdued hours of solitary meditation and prayer, when the heart communes with itself in the chamber and is still—then to turn to Jesus, and believe that He came "to seek and to save that which was lost," and that He is God,—this is the true, the unfailing ground of hope and joy. The very thought of the possibility of such mercy to remedy, and finally remove all the evil, rising up before the terrible vision of future woe denounced on sin—sin which could not otherwise be forgiven in this world, nor in the world to come—is the ground-work of enduring peace.

And when the Church of Christ would carry out the ministrations of truth and mercy committed to her, in preaching, in private warning, or in the more secret ministries of confession and absolution and spiritual guidance, it is not the Church that gives the hope and joy that is felt within, but the consciousness that God is behind the scene, within the ministry. His sympathy, His healing virtue is perceived as the inner spiritual grace of the outward form of the sacramental ordinance. He is still present, recognised as of old, though not in visible Substance, yet in power, in virtue, in actual Presence, though unseen, and in the full force of His redeeming, renewing love. The Penitent stretches out his hand, his heart, to touch, to hold, to cling to, His gracious Presence, Himself inwardly revealed, and feels the virtue flowing forth from Him as of old, when He visibly appeared, yea, more fully now, because His Spirit is shed abroad in our hearts to inspire and seal with secret indwelling grace all the ministrations of the Church.

Thus even now here on earth to the soul blighted by sin, amazed with fears, wrung with remorse, there is a sure hope of returning peace, and even of joy. The vigour of youth, and its buoyant spirits, may be broken down, never to be restored; the natural life lose all its freshness, all former pleasure cease to please, and the world no longer be what it once was, nor the zest with which its prizes were once pursued, be ever felt again; and there may be burdens strange and weary, and terrors casting their gloomy shadows over the soul, clouding all the future. Nevertheless there is hope, yea, there is an assurance, that a new spring of life may be felt within, and a new joy arise in the consciousness of reconciliation with God through the Atonement of Christ. "Blessed is he whose unrighteousness is forgiven, and whose sin is covered. Blessed is the man unto whom the Lord will not impute sin." It is a changed joy; the rising as of a new world of life, but it is the joy of the Spirit of God sealing the forgiveness and renewed love into which the soul of the reconciled Penitent has passed. As "there is joy in heaven over one sinner that repenteth," even so there is a reflection of this heavenly joy in the heart of the Penitent. He already tastes of the peace which passeth understanding. He is at rest in this new-found bliss. Moreover, there opens before his awakened spirit the hope of the yet higher joys now restored to him, as his rightful inheritance, if he fail not to preserve and follow the grace of his reconciliation,—the joy of the Lord, Who hath redeemed him, to be fulfilled in His own perfected kingdom of glory, "the pleasures which are at God's right hand for evermore."

Now unto Him who hath redeemed us, and hath washed us in His own blood, and hath made us unto our God, kings and priests, be glory and honour and thanksgiving for ever and ever. *Amen.*

SERMON VIII.

DAVID IN HIS SIN AND HIS PENITENCE.

BY

THE REV. E. B. PUSEY, D.D.

CANON OF CHRIST CHURCH, AND REGIUS PROFESSOR
OF HEBREW, OXFORD.

SERMON VIII.

PSALM LI. 4.

Against Thee, Thee only, have I sinned.

A BLOOD-STAINED saint! Surely, among all the mysteries of nature or of revelation there is but one, impenetrably, unfathomably, dark; of which reason has no solution, in which faith itself can see no light, except by looking beyond it to its God. And yet it surrounds us, presses upon us, is in us, of us; well is it if, by the grace of our God, it masters us not. All those mysteries, of which men have spoken so boldly, are light and light-giving. The mysteries as to God, what are they but the unfolding to us of something of His Being, which it shall be the bliss of Heaven to behold? There, the darkness is but the dazzling effulgence of His light. "Thou clothest Thyself with light as with a garment." All which we see is light. It is the light itself which, in this life, shrouds as yet the glories of His Deity. Mysteries as to God are but glimpses from His ineffable light. All from God is light, all which is darkness is from ourselves. The one dreadful, unfathomable mystery is sin. God created beings out of His Infinite love, that they might be for ever increasingly blessed in His love. He created all good, in grace. He offered Himself to their love; to the heavenly spirits, unveiled; to Adam, known, believed, but unseen. He willed to be chosen by the free-will of each. We know the result. His creatures could behold the All-Perfect, face to face, and could say, "I will not have Thee." This choice is sin. This choice every deadly sin has more or less consciously repeated. The creature rejects the Infinite Good, which is God, for something out of God. Satan chose to be first in hell rather than be all-but-first in heaven.

But since sin is this unutterable mystery, no wonder that we sinners misjudge well-nigh every thing connected with it. We weigh with unjust balances. The subjects of men's apologies have been those characters in Holy Scripture whom God rejected. The objects of their censure have been those whom God approved.

Strangely have Nathan's words been fulfilled, century after century: "Thou hast given great occasion to the enemies of the Lord to blaspheme." The heathen taunted us of old, "Lo how these Christians follow innocency, extol faith, venerate religion, teach chastity, whose princes appear to have committed homicides and adulteries. David himself, of whose line ye say Christ chose to be born, sang of his homicides and adulteries. What can the disciples be who have these for their masters[1]!" Modern blasphemy delights to blacken "the man after God's own heart." It *was* a terrific fall, terrible as well as piteous. In his youth, noble, chivalrous, generous, dauntless, tender to his relentless persecutor, "a heart of fire," to whom the love of Jonathan was wonderful, passing the love of women[2]. He, so tender, so forbearing; he whose heart smote him that he had a little shamed the enemy who sought his life, who passionately lamented Saul too, as lovely and pleasant; he who so hated wrong, who was so moved for the poor man's ewe-lamb, could this be he who had his own gallant soldier slain? He, so blameless in youth, could he, when life had begun to set, be stained so miserably through the passions of youth? I have said nothing. For I have spoken of nature only.

His inner life we know from his Psalms. What, when we know, that in God he laid him down to sleep, to God he woke; God he set alway before him, his eyes

[1] In S. Ambros. *Apol. David.* II. c. 3. [2] 2 Sam. i. 26.

ever turned toward his God? He knew the nothingness of all fleeting things, even the fullest store which God Himself could bestow in this life; and had chosen no created thing, but his God, for his portion, and the beatific vision of God, beyond the grave, for his inheritance, and meantime the sweet familiar intercourse with God, which God, he says, bestows on them that fear Him. His royal cares hindered not his meditating in the law of his God, day and night. He delighted to be humble before God, yet thought not that it was humility. He knew the frailty of nature, and prayed that presumptuous sins should not rule over him. He had reverent sympathy with the sufferings of his Redeemer, yet to come, and felt them as his own. All his Psalms bear witness to his one fixed will, that God and no created thing out of God should be his deliberate choice.

Yet these too were gifts of ordinary grace. What, when God had chosen him, not like Balaam, as the unwilling instrument of prophecy, but to attune his soul to the secret inspirations of His Spirit, that the Spirit of the Lord should speak by him, and His word be on his tongue, and should pour forth by him that wondrous, ever-varying, melody of thoughts from God to God, which have expressed the inmost longings of the soul for nearly 3000 years, which

Christian thought could expand, but has not yet exhausted, for it was God's word through man! God speaks to us in all His word; through David's Psalms we speak in God's own words to God. An inspired writer, and so deeply inspired (O horrible!), for one brief moment an adulterer and a murderer! Surely nothing can weary the condescension of our God, or the overwhelmingness of His grace, or the perseveringness of His love, Who chose to be called the Son of *him* who had so fallen, Who, obliterating what He gave the grace to repent of, still calls "the man after His own heart" him who "did right in His eyes, save in the matter of Uriah the Hittite." It is an intense mystery of sin, that man should admit so black a spot, where all around was so fair; it is an intenser mystery of God's love, that He should have arrested so black a spot from spreading and overcasting and infecting the whole. Yet now too, those conversant with human souls know something of that awful ever-watchful malice of Satan; how he delights, if he can, to precipitate a person, if but once, into a sin, foreign from the whole history of his soul before or after, and leave it stained and blighted with a sin foreign to its nature. The self-same cause is probably the occasion in both, false security. David says it of himself: "I said, I shall never be moved.

Thou didst turn Thy face from me and I was troubled." The Apostle says: "He that thinketh he standeth, let him take heed, lest he fall." To think himself secure is to fall at the next step. David was secure, careless, desired, hoped that it would not prove sin, that Bathsheba might be free. Then he had to give up his passion or his sin. He did not abide in his sin. She came, she went; outwardly he went on as before. Then came the dread of involving her in disgraceful death, and of his own shame. Then the attempt to deceive him whom he had injured, and lastly, the slaying him with the sword of the children of Ammon.

David's was the worse death. To part with the soul is the death of the body; the death of the soul is to part with God. It is to part with the life of grace, the light of grace, the union with God. It is to lose God. David, had he so continued, must have been like Cain, or like him who had the outward likeness of David's act in that he sold the innocent blood to His enemies, and went to his own place.

In one way, the sin was irremediable. It changed David's eternal condition. It is the terrific character of sin, that, though it may be, *as though* it had never been, God has made it to be self-contradictory, that what has been, should not have been. What we have been, *that* in all eternity, we must have been. God can forgive sin; He can be to us as if we had never sinned; perhaps He could, (although He does not,) obliterate the memory of sin in His forgiven ones; He can overwhelm it with the rich exuberance of His grace and love; He can (thanks be to Him) transform ourselves; He can and does re-create us, so that the sin should leave no trace on the soul, save that the soul hates it with a perfect hatred, and, through the Grace of God, will love, with the whole compass of its being, Him who forgave it. Redeeming, forgiving love, is our deepest joy here; to love Him who loved, and, loving, redeemed us, will be a joy of all eternity. God can re-make us. One thing Almighty love cannot undo; He cannot now (since it is self-contradictory) make it that the great penitent never should have sinned, as he did sin. David, like the blest Robber, the first fruits of the Redeeming Blood of Jesus, is, through those same merits, glorious with the indwelling glory of God; yet his soul, doubtless one of the highest of much-forgiven penitents, is still a soul, which, by two insulated acts, broke to the uttermost God's most sacred laws of purity and of love.

How then was he restored? Grace had been sinned away. He was left to his natural self. He had still those habits of mind, short of grace, which had been formed by grace. He had still that strong sense of justice, and hatred of the very sins by which he had fallen, which responded so quickly and so indignantly against cruelty and wrong, when called out by Nathan's parable. He must have had remorse. He was a man still; the wreck of a noble, ardent, generous man. The sight of the accomplice of his sin, who had been the occasion of his yet deeper sin, must often have recalled to him with agony, *whose* she once had been. With the news of the war there must have flashed before his eyes that phantom-form of his noble mighty one, ranked among his thirty faithful warriors, placed where the battle was hottest, fighting for him, forsaken by his orders, hemmed in, faithful unto death to him, the faithless. Remorse is the fruit of the most condescending love of our God. Neglected or stifled, it is the last grace by which God would save the soul; it is the first by which God would prepare the soul, which has forfeited grace, to return to Him. Precious, inestimable, in God's mercy almost inextinguishable grace, which God is so unwilling to withdraw, because it is the last hold which keeps His redeemed, while they are looking over and ready to cast themselves into the pit of hell. God sitteth within the soul, as its Judge; His voice speaks, and with power; He turns the soul in upon itself; the undeadened soul is its own incorruptible accuser, the witness against itself; its own executioner. Go where man will, he cannot leave himself; his guilty conscience is himself. If even love is extinct or asleep in the soul, it tells the soul, "Thou hast degraded thyself; thou art become like the beasts that perish; thou art not what thou wert, what thou shouldest be, what thou once longedst to be." If faith, though now an inoperative belief, is not altogether lost, it says, "Thou hast deserved hell;" and the cowering, tormented soul is forced to own, "I have."

But remorse, although a first step to repentance, is not repentance. For remorse centres in a man's self. It dreads the temporal penalty of its sin; it dreads more or less distinctly its deserved doom; it sees in the distance the fires of hell; it writhes at the thought of itself. While it is mere remorse, it does not turn to God. Cain had remorse, and accused God; Esau had remorse for his profane sale of his birthright, and purposed to regain it by fratricide; Ahab had remorse, did some great deeds of humble penitence, but died in his pride and rebellion; Judas had remorse, but hanged himself and went to his own place.

And so God, in His love, sent to him the prophet, the very sight of whom might recall to him the mercies of God in the past, His promises for the future, and the memory of those days of innocent service and bright aspirations, to which the soul, overtaken by sin, looks back with such sorrowful yearning. Nathan was the prophet who had accepted his purpose of building the temple, and when this was deferred, for the blood which had of necessity been shed in war, gave him those promises, which culminated in our Lord. How often now too will the sight of one, known in innocency, strike through the soul with the piercing,—it may be, by God's grace, converting—thought, "What was I once? what might I have been? what am I now?" You know how, by enlisting his better feelings, Nathan predisposed him for grace, and then heaped on the head of the convicted sinner those coals of fire, the accumulated forecoming mercies of his God, who had daily laden him with benefits, and would have given him more than all which his heart could crave, had he sought it from Him, not against Him. The heavy stone, which lay on the choked dead heart, was rolled away; the dead was alive again, the two-edged sword of God's word, Judgment and Mercy, had slain him to himself that he might live to God. The awakened soul burst out in those two words[1], "I have sinned against the Lord."

[1] חטאתי ליהוה.

Then was remorse absorbed, transformed, spiritualised into penitent love. The relation of the creature to its Creator was restored. I, Thou! All else had vanished before him, as it shall at the Day of Judgment. He who had foretold the good to David's house, had now foretold its woe. "The sword shall never depart from thy house." David is as though he heard it not. One thought filled his soul; one sight alone he saw. "I have betrayed, been faithless to, have sinned against my God." That thought, that sight, never departed from him. His first gush of penitence lived on more vividly in his great penitential Psalm. "Against Thee, Thee only have I sinned." What? had he not sinned against Uriah? Yes! Penitence does not extenuate guilt, but it sees it all, where, in contrast with the All-Perfect Holiness, it looks most terrible, in God. His brave soldier was dead. Reparation there was none. The sword of the sons of Ammon had removed to Abraham's bosom the faithful Hittite, adopted into the one family of God. He does not say *as to* whom he had sinned, but *to* Whom; to Whom he was amenable, Who was the centre at which all sin is aimed, as all good is directed towards Him; Whose love the sword, which slew Uriah, wounded; Who Alone could condemn him, because He was sinless; against Whom Alone his own special evil lay, because He was All-Good. It was nothing to him, although the whole world, his fellow-sinners, should lessen his sin to him, that they should make those pleas, so readily made for the great; that they should not dare to condemn, being themselves self-condemned as sinners. The whole world, with its praise or blame, its acquittal or its condemnation, is as if it were not, an utter blank to the soul which, face to face, stands before its Maker and its God. "Against Thee have I sinned, Who madest me in Thine own image; against Thee Who, in all eternity, didst love me infinitely and didst make me, because Thou lovedst me; against Thee, Who didst will that I should be a little created likeness of Thy perfections; not a microcosm, but a little god upon earth, goddized by the presence of God. Against Thee, Who all my life long didst tend me with such individual love, as if in all Thy creation Thou hadst none besides to love; Who didst enlighten, engladden, engrace, inspiritualise me; Who didst place, yea hide me in Thine own Presence, and admit me to the secret intercourse of a friend. Against Thee, such in Thyself, such towards me, I have sinned."

And what is sin? What is it to own that one

has sinned? What is it but to own one's self guilty of the basest, blackest, shamefullest ingratitude, of which, were it shewn to a fellow-sinner, one could never lift up one's head again? What is it, but to charge our God with want of wisdom or of love, that He forbade us those things, which we did against His All-Holy will? What is it, but to wish that God were other than He is, less holy, less good, less just, less righteous, less perfect? What is it but to wish to unmake God, as He is, and to make us a god, such as we are, who could take pleasure in our foulnesses, and in us so foul? "Thou thoughtest," saith God, "that I was even such an one as thyself." Wilful sin is to tell God, the only good, to His Face, "On Thy own terms I will have none of Thee. I prefer this and this and this to Thee."

Bitter it is for a sinner to awaken from his stupor, and to own all this to himself and to his God. And thence all those lying excuses to hide the black spot, if one could, to cover it with our half-transparent hands, and tell God, "it is not there: He was mistaken in calling it sin, we did but follow our nature, such as He made us."

Bitter it is to own that we have parted with God, unfitted ourselves for His Holy Presence, defiled our souls, lied to our consciences, mocked at grace, despised the glorious end of our being, condemned ourselves to everlasting severance from God, exchanged the goodness of our God for Satan's hateful mastery.

And since it is so hard and bitter a thing to own this, therefore it is the greater grace to own without reserves, without excuses, not hiding, like Adam, our sin, how we have worse than fallen from heaven to hell; for "better were it, free from sin, to enter hell—than, defiled by sin, to enter the kingdom of Heaven." Better were it! for, with God, hell were heaven; without God, heaven were hell.

And so those words, "I have sinned against the Lord," had such transforming power. For it was the grace of God, translating the soul from darkness to light, from the power of Satan unto God. The closed heart was opened; the corroding poison was cast out; the soul was of one mind with God; the love of God made the memory of sin a channel of Divine Grace.

But this was the beginning of the renewed life of the soul, not the end. It issued in a constant longing for a re-creation, a reverent fear springing from the sense of what it had deserved, an earnest craving for a more thorough cleansing from every stain or spot of sin, a thirst for the purging by the atoning

Blood, an unvarying sight of His forgiven sinfulness, spreading far and wide from the core of original sin, a longing to do free noble generous service, and all, from God to God, from God's re-creating, renewing, enfreedoming, ennobling grace.

A little of David's soul we see in his acceptance of God's thickening chastisements, his meek bearing of Shimei's curses, his accepting them as the voice of God declaring his deserts, his prompt forgiveness. It is as if he had heard the words, "Forgive as thou wouldest be forgiven." It is one offering of himself on each occasion to God, "Burn, cut here, and spare for ever." He was "very wroth" at Amnon's violation of nature; but he was still. *He* had been an adulterer. Absalom fled after his fratricide. David restored him. He charged his captains to deal tenderly with the parricide son, before whom he had fled. He himself had been a murderer. Where was the fiery spirit which had so resented Nabal's churlishness? The sword, which slew Uriah, had, through God's grace, pierced his own soul. Well might the poor father wish he had died for the unnatural son whom his own example had taught deadly offences against purity and the life of man, and who, as far as man knew, had died impenitent in his sin, and, if so, had died the second death. The broken and contrite heart cannot crush an offence against itself.

But far more deeply do David's Psalms lay open his inmost soul. For they are the words, which God the Holy Ghost gave him, the "unutterable groanings," which the Holy Spirit embodied in words, which have been the voice of penitents ever since, and shall be, until the number of God's elect shall be accomplished, the vacant thrones in His many mansions shall be filled, and the sounds of penitence shall be transfigured into the jubilee of forgiven love. "Unutterable" were those "groanings," though uttered. We hear the words; we know their meaning; they express our poor penitence; but there is a depth of sorrow below, which human heart has perhaps never fathomed, which, when we have learned something of God-given sorrow for sin, is still beyond the compass of our souls. The words express our sorrow; they teach us how to express it to God; but there is a deep base of mourning sorrow which our poor voices do not fill. It is the Divine Dove, teaching the penitent, through the great penitent, how to moan for sin. It tells us that sorrow for having displeased our good loving God is, in this life, inexhaustible. We learn it, as we learn every grace, by opening our souls to receive from God what in its whole compass is unattainable.

And this sorrow was not that first stunning crushing sense of sin, which the erring soul has on its first conversion. The deepest of David's Psalms of penitence express the sorrow for forgiven sin. Once he tells us, how it was with him, while the sense of his guilt was upon him, ere he confessed it to God. "While I kept silence, my bones wore away through my roaring all the day long. For day and night Thy hand was heavy upon me; my life's sap was changed into the drought of summer[1]." But those wearying groanings, those nightly tears, with which, night by night, he made his bed to swim; that eye-consuming grief[2]; that suffering within and without, when the hand of God pressed him down, his own sins passed as it were over his prostrated soul[3]; and he was "writhed," "bowed[4]," "congealed[5]," "crushed[5]," "sightless[6]," "strengthless[6]," "fleshless[7]," "scorched[8]," "withered[9]," "heart-stricken[10]," were, when he was forgiven; he had known his forgiveness from the voice of God Himself by His Prophet. Yet more. David had

[1] Ps. xxxii. 3, 4.
[2] Ps. vi. 6, 7, 8.
[3] Ps. xxxviii. 2, 4.
[4] Ib. 6.
[5] Ib. 9. Heb.
[6] Ib. 11. Heb.
[7] Ps. cii. 5.
[8] Ps. xxxviii. 8. Heb.; cii. 3.
[9] Ps. vi. 3. Heb.; cii. 4.
[10] Ps. cii. 4.

been secure once, and had fallen terribly. He never was secure again. He had a reverent fear that he might lose God. He could bear the thought, because God sustained him, and he clung to his God. Still the thought, the prayer was there, "Cast me not, fling me not away from standing in Thy presence." Once, but for God's overwhelming grace, he had been lost for ever. Had the messenger of death been sent then, when Uriah was slain, before even the fulfilled sin had brought its remorse! Like the penitent of the Gospel, after his Father had received him, he still said, "I am no more worthy to be called Thy son." Still he prayed, "For Thy tender mercy's sake fling me not away." David knew of that place, where there was no remembrance of God[1]. He had known God, as his own God; he knew what it had been to be without God; and he dreaded, as the most intolerable of all agonies, the endless loss of God and the beatific vision of God, hopeless for ever.

Then David knew the "stain" of sin. O that deep, ingrained, intolerable, ineffaceable stain of sin, which would whole seas incarnadine, which nothing can wash out but the Sacred Blood of Christ. Yet this too not at once. The sin is forgiven at once: the eternal penalty is remitted, but its effects remain

[1] Ps. vi. 5.

"scourges in our sides and thorns in our eyes," which God in His mercy leaves to goad us on to more devoted exertion; spectres of past sins, which haunt us; hateful thoughts, their genuine offspring, ready to storm our momentary consent; a chill cold mist clinging to us, pressing in upon us and numbing our energies for God, weaknesses, confusion of motives, tongue-tied cowardice in the cause of God. And since evil is only displaced by grace, he prays for a re-creation. "Create in me a new heart." He uses the word, whereby God speaks of the creation of the heaven and the earth. For greater and more joyous is the re-creation of one sinner that repenteth, than of the whole sidereal system. "Wash me mightily from my sin; let a mighty perennial stream of mercy wash away the mightiness of transgression."

But pardon, cleansing, justifying, renewing, sufficed not David; they content not the penitent. Whoso has been upon the brink of Hell, whoso knows that he has deserved to be flung away from God's presence, whoso has known the value of a soul by the peril of his own, would not be saved alone, if indeed any, except in some extremity of long-suffering, could be saved alone.

And so, with that re-creation, he prays for that promptness of heart, ever impulsive, or rather grace-impelled, to princely[1], generous service, which should teach sinners the ways of God, and be saved with a multitude of returning souls.

Such was, in summary, David's penitence, a restful, never-resting sorrow, for the love of God, that it had displeased God; self-mistrustful, God-trusting; ever-longing to be cleansed more and more by the Atoning Blood, to be re-created, renewed by the Divine Spirit, ever thirsting for the salvation of sinners, that his fellows in sin might be his fellow-penitents. Strange contrast with our smooth ways of would-be repentance, which tells God in an easy way, that it has done what it ought not, and so makes it up with God, and goeth its way, and straightway forgetteth what manner of man it was. Which then was the right? Judge your own selves. Natural is it to shrink from the sight of remembered sin. For it has a countenance more terrible than Hell. Natural were it, if to forget it were to efface it. Yet I speak not now of grace or revelation; I ask which was truest to our better nature, to our human feelings. Picture to thyself one who was to thee as thine own soul, who had loved thee, yearned and watched over thee with the love of a tenderest mother, and, I say not, picture thyself (thou couldest not do it), but picture every in-

[1] Ps. li. 14. Heb.

gratitude shewn towards her, her children suffering every evil of soul and body at the hands of him, whom, together with them, she had ever tenderly cherished! Suppose such an one fully forgiven, overwhelmed with fresh love. Could he forget what he had done? Could he, in fullest, most undoubting possession of her love, not reproach himself the more, not repent the more? Could he weary of shewing how deeply he repented? What were the love of the tenderest mother to the tender yearning love of Almighty God? Thy mother bore thee. God, in His eternal love, created thee for Himself, for His love. Thy mother might die for thee, she could not redeem thee; too precious is the price of thy soul[1]. God gave His Son to be incarnate and to die for thee, as much as if in the whole world there had been none beside for whom to be crucified. God cared for thee day by day; day by day, and hour by hour, thy Saviour interceded; yea at this moment He intercedeth for thee. God the Holy Ghost ever warned thee against thy sin, never wearied of knocking at thy heart.

This is He against whom we sinners sinned. If our sin ever injured another, was ever committed with another, by word or deed, they were His sons and daughters, against whom we sinned: in them we

[1] Ps. xlix. 7, 8.

sinned against Him. It is He who says, "When ye sin so against the brethren—ye sin against Christ." Men speak of David's sin. Might not the faithful prophet rise up in the midst of this church, and, to any one who had injured another's soul, say more terrifically, "Thou art the man." The murder of the body may be but the passport to heaven. The murder of the soul is Satan's own act, the plunging into Hell. Have we love? Have we fear? Have we hearts, that they should not break at wounding such love, with the crushing weight of such guiltiness?

We have been wiser than God. We found it joyous to dwell on the goodness of our God, and the love of Christ, and the sweet communion through the Spirit, and we thought that the love of Christ would alone constrain men to love Him, and we shrank from contemplating the horrors of hell. And so the unpreached doctrine slipped out of men's practical Creeds, and we are startled to find that the suppressed doctrine was denied, imperilled, though, in God's mercy, not yet forfeited. And we have lukewarm repentance, and easy ways, and tampering with sin, and opiates for the conscience, and stuntedness in spiritual growth, and giant thanklessness. We have a sensual, debased population, and hard rocky hearts against our brethren's cry and need.

Fear of Hell drives men to repentance, fear of Hell quickens repentance, for it intensifies the love for the Redeemer. Never will men feel the all-but infinite evil and hatefulness of sin save in the sight of Hell and of their Redeemer from Hell. Not for any slight cause did God become man. Not for any slight cause were those awful sufferings, which exsuded those drops of Blood, or called forth that loud Cry upon the Cross. God, become Man to die for men, and that unutterable woe, are awful awful counterparts.

Let not men deceive you in the Name of God. Trust God with His own creation. Think if there is any way, in which that awful truth of the eternity of woe could have been taught, in which God has not taught it. Think Who revealed the sinner's hell, Whose lips, full of grace, spoke of its being better never to have been born[1], of the whole body being cast into hell[2]; Who bid us fear Him which is able to destroy both body and soul in hell[3]; Who told us so often of the furnace of fire and the outer darkness where is weeping and gnashing of teeth[4]; Who warned us of losing our souls[5], Who spake

[1] S. Matth. xxvi. 24.
[2] S. Matth. v. 29, 30; xviii. 8.
[3] S. Matth. x. 28; S. Luke xii. 4.
[4] S. Matth. xiii. 42, 50, &c.; viii. 12, &c.
[5] S. Matth. xvi. 26; S. Mark viii. 36.

of *their* worm and *their* fire, their own special suffering as undying and unextinguishable[1];—and think whether He or man would deceive you.

Men accuse God, while they flatter Him. They call it blasphemy against the love of God to say that He could sentence any to eternal woe. It is against Thee, our Redeemer, that they renew the accusation of Thine enemies on earth, "Thou blasphemest." For Thou didst teach it us. And if Thou, the Truth, the true Light, Eternal Love, deceivedst not, then men who say that Thou taughtest pious frauds for our good, that Thou didst use in ambiguous senses, side by side, the self-same word of everlasting life, and everlasting fire, knowing or ignorant that there was no fire which lasts for ever, blaspheme Thee. Forgive them, Lord, who forgavest Thine executioners.

No, my brother, my son, bow your minds for this little while to the intensity of this dread mystery. Dare to look at Hell, and read there our own deserts, and how God must have loved thy free love and choice of Himself, that, at the risk of losing thee, He endowed thee with that nobility of choice, to choose Himself.

[1] S. Mark ix. 44, 46, 48; cf. Isai. lxvi. 24. See "Litany of our Lord's Warnings," by the Rev. J. Keble.

Gaze on the Blood-stained Form, that meek Eye of love, those outstretched racked arms on Calvary; hark to that loud piercing cry of superhuman agony, "My God, my God, why hast Thou forsaken Me?" But that thou mayest understand what man can imagine of that dread Agony, the blackness of sin and of its ingratitude, look down on hell. The thought of both, of Him who saved thee, and from what He saved thee, will by His grace, be the best preservative against deadly sin.

If thou hast fallen grievously, there thou wilt learn the black hatefulness of thine own deadly sin, for which God could choose no other lot; there thou wilt learn the infinity of thy Redeemer's love; there, to cling closer to His Cross; there, to bear thankfully the little sufferings which He lays upon thee; there, to dread the slightest incursion of sin; there, to shake off this apathy which numbs us, that we know not what is burning love for souls or fiery zeal or self-sacrificing piety, and pass by on the other side, while our brother perishes; there thou wilt learn that it is more than the whole world, yea than a thousand worlds, to be His instrument of saving even if it be but one soul; there wilt thou learn to ask of Him who will give it thee, true repentance, meek reverence, loving faith; and He who died to save thee will extinguish for thee the fires of Hell ; and that awful doom from which He saved thee will but deepen the depth of the God-given, God-sustained, God-enabled love, wherewith thou wilt eternally love, eternally praise, Him who loved thee and gave Himself for thee.

SERMON IX.

GOD THE CONSOLATION OF THE AFFLICTED.

BY

THE VERY REVEREND

WALTER FARQUHAR HOOK, D.D., F.R.S.

DEAN OF CHICHESTER,
AND CHAPLAIN IN ORDINARY TO THE QUEEN.

SERMON IX.

LAMENTATIONS III. 32, 33.

Though He cause grief, yet will He have compassion according to the multitude of His mercies. For He doth not afflict willingly nor grieve the children of men.

THE prophet Jeremiah was one of the most afflicted of mankind. He was afflicted in himself, his family, his church, his country. We have his Lamentations in the book from which our text is taken. From that book we learn, that for affliction man is permitted to grieve; and that he may give utterance to his feelings of grief, in order that he may enjoy that mysterious consolation and comfort, which, whether we can account for it or not, the social nature of man finds and is intended to find in sympathy.

Afflictions are sent to make us grieve; and all

that is required of us, whether in grief or in joy, is moderation.

How to moderate our grief we learn from this inspired book of the prophet Jeremiah. The prophet, under inspiration, is permitted to give vent to his feelings, and to refer to those many topics of consolation, which revealed religion suggests to the sanctified mind; topics, which received, of course, additional lustre and force, as new facts were, from time to time, revealed, until in a completed Bible miraculous revelation ceased.

The subject, upon which I propose to enlarge this day, is the consolation, which in our sufferings and sorrows we cannot fail to derive, when we realise it to our minds, from the fact, that God doth not willingly afflict the children of men;—that, in His sterner visitations, He always has some ulterior object in view, in which our own eventual and eternal welfare is nearly concerned.

I have stated a revealed fact: God doth not willingly afflict the children of men.

This fact rests upon another fact; and can only become consolatory when we have formed some definite notion of what the Scriptures teach us of the Providence of God.

We are taught in Scripture, that the things of this

world, temporal and spiritual, are ordered by the joint agency of God and man; God having endowed His intellectual creation, and, among them, man, with the high prerogative of being fellow-helpers with Omnipotence. Or we may rather attribute the progress of events to the Divine agency, acting through a general, and through a particular and special Providence.

According to the general Providence of God, certain laws, discovered, or more or less discoverable, have been established—the laws of nature. It is by an observance of these laws, that man is to obtain, to a certain extent, what he desires to possess. He sees that, within certain limits, he has control over events; and consequently, he sees the necessity of exertion. He is to exercise his mind, that the best means may be devised for the accomplishment of his ends, and he is to labour diligently and with self-denial in the course prescribed.

But although, according to the general Providence of God, the battle is to the strong and the race to the swift, it, nevertheless, so frequently happens, that the converse is true, that the wise man, having admitted the general law, exclaims with astonishment, "I returned and saw under the sun that the race is *not* to the swift, nor the battle to the strong, neither yet bread to the wise, nor riches to men of understanding, nor yet favour to men of skill—but time and chance happeneth to all."

By chance is meant not, of course, an uncaused event, but an event the immediate cause of which is not discoverable by man. And why? Even because with the constituted order of things God Himself doth directly, or through the instrumentality of undiscoverable or unusual causes, interfere.

He has set the universe in motion as a great machine; but He has not left it to its own working. If it be a mighty machine, it is a machine, still under the controlling hand and influence of the Creator's power and mind.

And this is the great doctrine of a particular and special Providence—which is the sole ground of prayer; prayer being the basis of all true religion.

We *pray* in vain unless we exert ourselves, whether in regard to things spiritual, or to things temporal, because, by the fact of our not exerting ourselves, we shew that we have no faith in the general Providence of God; that we set at nought the order of things which He, in His wisdom, has appointed and ordained. On the other hand, we *labour* in vain, in things temporal as well as things spiritual, unless we also pray; because by our neglect of prayer we indicate a want of faith in the particular Providence of God.

When once the mind has been habituated to dwell upon that special Providence of God, which brings the laws of a general Providence to bear upon our own particular case, it gradually learns the more difficult task of submitting to all afflictive dispensations, with thanksgiving; and to regard the human being, through whose wickedness we have been robbed, traduced, or wronged, as only a rod in our Heavenly Father's hand. So that when, notwithstanding our exertions and our prayers, through an order of events we have been unable to control, we have been chilled by disappointment, or involved in ruin, we look up and say, It is the Lord, let Him do as seemeth unto Him good; what has been done and endured will only minister to my greater glory in that mansion, which my Saviour is preparing for me, and for which I am myself in a state of preparation. What I suffer I know to be absolutely necessary; or these sufferings I should not be called upon to undergo; for my God hath declared that He doth not afflict willingly, that is, except for some ulterior object, the children of men.

Though He cause grief, yet will He have compassion, according to the multitude of His mercies.

For He doth not afflict willingly or grieve the children of men.

We further remark on this passage, that, at first sight, it appears to stand opposed to an attribute of the great and good God—His Omnipotence.

I remark this the rather, because it is by logical though unauthorised deductions from the revealed word of God, that, in all ages, men have been led into much religious error, and into infidelity itself. If God be what He reveals Himself to be, then it is assumed that such and such consequences must inevitably ensue. And this, though the conclusion plainly contradicts some other attribute equally a subject of revelation.

"The truth lies," says St Chrysostom, "in a strict and narrow way, between two steep precipices: and there is reason to fear lest, while we contend successfully against the one sort of heretics, we ourselves be wounded by the other. For, if we assert the unity of the Godhead, immediately Sabellius draws that expression to his own impious sense. Again; if we make a distinction, and say the Father is one, the Son another, the Holy Ghost another, Arius is ready to wrest that distinction of persons into a difference of substance. And it equally concerns us to avoid the impious confusion of the one and the mad diversity of the other, by confessing the Godhead of the Father, Son, and Holy Ghost, to be all one, and by adding thereto a Trinity of persons; for thus we shall fortify ourselves against the assaults of both[1]."

So we say God is Almighty; and yet, throughout the Scripture, we find that there are things God cannot do,—cannot, in the same sense in which we say that a good man cannot lie or steal. As man, he can do both; but if he be guilty of either, he ceases to be a good man. God, as God, can do all things; but, as the Sovereign Ruler of the universe, there are some things He cannot do, for to do them would be to depose Himself. It is on this account, that we commence the Creed with the article, which says, I believe in God the Father Almighty. This, in the mouth of an unbeliever in revelation, would be a mere truism, which it were needless to utter. In the mouth of a Christian it means: — Although the Scriptures teach us that there are some things which God cannot do, nevertheless I believe God to be Almighty. This is one of what Bacon calls the paradoxes of Christianity.

The whole Christian scheme, the scheme of salvation, rests upon this fact; and it is from not having realised this fact, that many reject the salvation

[1] *De Sacerdotio*, Lib. IV. § 4.

offered to the perishing sons of men, in Christ Jesus our Lord.

The Lord God Almighty, God the Blessed Trinity, in the infinity of His bounty, willed creation, and commanded rational beings into existence: not man only, but angels and archangels, the principalities and powers, called the hosts of heaven; some of them dwelling, with the elements of all things, in the atmosphere around us. Of these intelligences, some of them are endowed with powers higher than those possessed by man, others probably are lower, in the scale of intellectual existence, than ourselves. But all are endowed with reason. Reason implies freedom of will. Freedom of will implies the power of the creature to say, I will not, when God saith, Thou shalt;—the tremendous power to disobey God,—to place the will of the creature, in opposition to the will of the Creator. But two wills cannot predominate. If the will of the creature—supposing it possible—were to triumph over the will of the Creator, the object of Satan would be accomplished, the universe would become an universal hell.

Since this could not be, a law was implied, in the very fact of there being created intelligences,—"Obey and live,—bend the created will to the will of the Creator, and happiness will be the result."

But a law implies not only a lawgiver, but a supreme magistrate to enforce its observance. Hence the Creator was revealed to His rational creation, in a new character,—that of the Sovereign Ruler of the universe.

And here at once we see, that the Almighty willed to set limits to the exercise of His Omnipotence. A ruler, even if it be he, who hath given the law, must himself abide by its terms, when once it has been enacted. And God, therefore, though Almighty, could not, as the Sovereign Ruler of the universe, King of Kings, and Lord of Lords, pardon the offender by a mere fiat of His will. The law connected life and happiness with obedience. But the law would cease to exist, if life and happiness were dispensed also to the disobedient.

Under this dispensation man was created; a rational being, who was to pass—through temptation—to a closer communion with God, than that which even the angels enjoy. But the will of man was, when tried,—the will of man, even now, is, when tried, as for instance by disappointment, shame or sorrow, opposed to the will of God.

How could he be rescued from the inevitable consequences of disobedience? Only by a miracle. A miracle might be once wrought in his favour; for a miracle would cease to be a miracle if repeated. A miracle of mercy was therefore decreed in the counsels of the Sacred Three,—by the infinite mercy of the One and Only God.

God, although Almighty, could not, as the Sovereign Ruler not of man only but the other hosts of His rational creation, relax the penalty of the law, unless something were first done, equivalent to the destruction of the human race, for upholding the majesty of the law. That the majesty of the law should be upheld, this the good of all required. God is Love. Love to the created intelligences, who had not sinned, required that the law should be maintained in the fulness of its supremacy; and so the law was magnified, beyond the conception of the highest of created intelligences, when God Himself yielded obedience to it.

But God, in Himself, as God, could not obey or disobey; therefore God in the Second Person of the Godhead assumed the human nature,—a nature in which he *could* obey.

Without ceasing to be God, God, in the Second Person of the Godhead, became man also: and the God-man, the Lord Jesus Christ, was tempted, tried —obeyed. He obeyed in all things, He obeyed even unto death; and although, in every act of His obedience there was an atoning efficacy, by His death the atonement was completed and our Salvation was accomplished.

Heaven is now re-opened to our race, because God was not willing that any should perish. But what is heaven? Heaven is a prepared place for a prepared people. And how are we to be prepared? How but by being disciplined to heavenly-mindedness.

And to discipline us, the Lord God Almighty presents Himself to the redeemed in Christ our Lord, in the character of a Father. The object of a good father is to promote the real and permanent happiness of his child. His happiness as far as possible now—and therefore he is not opposed to childish sports,—but not his present happiness only or chiefly. He looks forward to his prosperity, his usefulness, and his fair fame in after life. For this, he trains him in habits of morality, religion, and industry; for this he corrects his faults, and encourages him in all his struggles after excellence. For this, he is warned in Scripture not to spare the rod,—not to fear, though he acts unwillingly, to inflict punishment when deserved.

It is our privilege when by faith we are one with Christ, the eternal Son of God, to regard the great God as our Father which is in heaven, and with filial confidence to expect from Him, the kind of treatment which from a good father every son receives. In other words, when we are once believers in the Lord Jesus, we become objects of the special Providence of God. Our heavenly Father will discipline us upon earth, that we may be prepared for heaven. But the same principle is observable.

He will not by His Omnipotence overrule or supersede the freedom of will, with which we are endowed. And if we be not true to ourselves, He will, at length, after trial, leave us to our own devices. He will cast us off, disinherit us. He Himself has told us in the first chapter of the book of Proverbs, "Because ye set at nought all my counsel and would none of my reproof, I also will laugh at your calamity, I will mock when your fear cometh, when your fear cometh as desolation, and your destruction cometh as a whirlwind; when distress and anguish cometh upon you; they shall call upon me, but I will not answer: they shall seek me, but they shall not find me."

It is indeed an awful thought that a man may outlive the day of grace. He may remain a *thing* upon earth to subserve some purpose in the Providence of God; but as a *person*, his trial may have ceased.

But we will not dwell upon an extreme case; we

will only remark, that if one of the purposes of affliction is to correct and amend in us, whatsoever may offend the eyes of our Father, Which is in Heaven; one of the means of avoiding affliction must be an honest endeavour to shape our lives according to the law of God. We do not say that you will thus escape affliction, for, as we shall presently shew, that the uses of adversity are manifold. But certainly, this is one of the means, to which a wise man will have recourse; when believing that all things are ordered by the Providence of God, and that God doth not willingly afflict the children of men, he is under the conviction, that whatever occurs, all things are ordered for their good to them that love the Lord Jesus.

What I have rather now to do, is to remind you of the ineffable consolation which, when afflictions *do* come, the Christian derives from this faith, this filial confidence in our God. God is indeed the consoler of His people, when having inspired His people with faith, they can hear His voice amidst the tempest and the storm:—It is I, be not afraid.

It has been in wisdom and in mercy, ordered that, in order to prevent our sitting in judgment upon others, we can never know, at the time of suffering, the precise object of the affliction with which we have been visited.

But the case is different when the subject is viewed historically; when we have laid open to us the life of a sufferer; and what, in his life, have been his constraining motives.

One of the advantages, which we possess in the Scriptures of the Old Testament is this:—that therein the veil between the visible and invisible is often raised; and we are permitted actually to see, what, under ordinary circumstances, we can only surmise,—the mysterious workings of a controlling Providence.

Under the Christian dispensation we possess a completed Bible, to which no additions can be made, and from which we are, by the exercise of reason, to make the necessary moral deductions.

In the infancy and boyhood of our race, it was different. Neither the Patriarchal nor the Levitical Church had a completed Bible. If then there were to be a revealed religion at those times, it could only be through a miraculous interposition on the part of God. This interposition took place, in the patriarchal Church, through the Jehovah Angel,—manifestations of the Second Person in the Godhead, the Word, which in the beginning was with God and was God,—the Person through whom, the invisible is made manifest. In the Jewish Church, this intervention took place, from time to time, through the miraculous inspiration of the prophets.

When we desire, therefore, to become acquainted with the workings of Divine Providence, it is to the ancient Scriptures, where these miraculous interpositions occur, that we more especially have recourse.

I propose to illustrate our present subject, by a reference to the history of some of those great men of our race, of whom, for this very purpose, a record has been preserved. We see them afflicted by Him who doth not willingly afflict the children of men,—and it is revealed to us why these afflictions were imposed upon them.

We will take first the history of Jacob.

Jacob is presented to us as a man of undoubted piety. He believed in Jehovah: in Jehovah he trusted; his loyalty to his God was unimpeached and unimpeachable. He looked forward, in the faith of the Patriarchal Church, to the time, when the Redeemer, promised to Adam, should stand upon the earth. He believed, as a necessary consequence, that, as the Patriarchal Creed is given in Job, the dead in the Lord should rise to share in the blessings which were to ensue from the Redeemer's coming. Faith in the Redeemer involved faith in the Resurrection. To be the progenitor of the Redeemer became, in his mind, through the vitality of his faith, an ambition.

But what was his history? We have spoken of the afflictions of Jeremiah; they were surpassed by the afflictions of Jacob. A combination of sorrows greater than that which made Jacob an old man before his time, it is scarcely possible to conceive.

A youth he was, of simple tastes; not like his brother a lover of adventure, a sportsman, a warrior. In Scripture phrase, he loved to dwell in tents. He (like his father) would go forth into the fields at eventide, there to meditate; and to enjoy the peaceful pleasures of a contemplative life, such as he hoped to lead.

We mention his natural disposition, because this rendered his exile the more calamitous; when, to avoid the just anger of his brother, he was compelled to leave his happy home; his father whose tastes were congenial with his own,—the mother he so dearly loved.

With a staff only for his protection, he had to traverse inhospitable regions; he had at last to dwell in a foreign land, and become little better than a bondslave in his kinsman's house. Hard tasks were imposed upon him, and his remuneration was begrudged. After twenty years of servitude, he was denied his due, and beguiled of his hope.

According to the custom of the land, what he could not pay in money, he earned by labour, a dower for his wife. And then when the dower was earned, instead of obtaining the object of his affections, he was defrauded into a marriage with Leah. When, at the price of an additional servitude, he at last obtained the hand of Rachel, she was for a season childless, and after the birth of her second son, Jacob wept tears of agony at her grave.

Having escaped the tyranny of Laban, his timid spirit quailed before his brother Esau, whom he had wronged; and when he escaped the peril of his brother's vengeance, and returned to his native land, they were dead, for a reunion with whom, his kind heart, through his long years of distant labour yearned. In the land of promise, he dwelt a stranger. The disputes, the jealousies, the iniquities of his children nearly brought his gray hairs with sorrow to the grave. He was filled with horror by the enormity of Reuben's sin. By the perfidy and cruelty of Simeon and Levi, his endeavours to conciliate the natives of Canaan were rendered nugatory. He had to deplore the dishonour of his daughter Dinah. Joseph, his beloved, the firstborn of his Rachel, was taken from him; his fate being the more deplorable because involved in mystery. His family was on the point of extinction from the want of food; and Benjamin was wrung from him.

Under all these awful afflictions, his spirit was bowed down, and (on his going into Egypt) he said to Pharaoh, that few and evil his days had been.

It was thus, that our Heavenly Father shewed favour to the son He loved. These were the blessings (for blessings they were) vouchsafed to the patriarch Jacob. Jacob had defrauded his brother; he had lied to his father; he fled like a coward, alarmed at the probable consequences of his conduct; he resorted to artifice to cheat his father-in-law: he wronged his other children, by the partiality he shewed to the sons of Rachel. A mean, a crafty, a sordid, a selfish disposition he had by nature. But he was affectionate, tender-hearted, full of devotional fervour. His ends were often righteous, though, to accomplish them, he had recourse to unrighteous means. And God dealt with him as with a son. He did not willingly afflict him; but because chastisement was necessary, he chastised him. Other agents were employed, but God used them as the rod in His hands. It was by an accumulation of afflictions only, that such a character could be reformed; that a tree so early bent in the wrong direction, through the training of a deceitful mother, could be made to stand upright:

It was by the furnace only, that from the gold, seen in his character by the all-searching eye, the dross could be purged, and gradually drawn off. He who loved to deceive, was throughout his life a victim to the deceit of others.

When affliction had done its work, then the lash of the scourge was no more inflicted; and the last seventeen years of the Patriarch's life were passed, though not in honour, yet in peace.

From what a complication of misery, my younger Brethren, you may possibly save yourselves, if only you will remember the Lord in the days of your youth; and so render chastening needless, from One who doth not afflict willingly, or grieve the children of men, by disciplining yourselves in the ways of godliness.

Nevertheless, afflictions are sent not only to correct and amend in us, whatsoever doth offend the eyes of our heavenly Father: they may be sent to train us, to educate us, to prepare us for elevation and honour in this world. Let us advert to the history of Jacob's greater son.

Joseph was noble, generous, openhearted, pure-minded, just, pious, and devout. His character was the converse of that of his father; and yet how many and grievous were his afflictions. At an early period of life he was torn from the home of his affections, from a too indulgent father; from a younger brother, his mother's son, over whom he watched with more than fraternal, almost with parental love; over whom he prayed, "God be gracious unto thee, my son." Through the treachery of envious brothers, all the hopes, around which his thoughts of the future had clustered, were dashed to the ground. He was sold a bond-slave. When his conduct was blameless, his character was traduced; he was calumniated, imprisoned. It is easy to say all this; but when we think what these things really were, and ask ourselves how we should have borne them, we see how really great his afflictions were.

Such was the man whom God, not willing to afflict the children of men, had predestined to be the viceroy of Egypt; that when for the sins of the people a famine was sent, there might be means of avoiding its misery, provided for the penitent few. Joseph was, in the counsels of God, predestined to be the foremost man in all the civilized world. He was to be a saviour and protector of his own perishing family, as well as a benefactor to the whole family of man.

And was a poor shepherd boy of a wandering tribe in Palestine prepared for such an exaltation as this? Is not a previous education required for the competent discharge of the duties attached to a high and responsible office? Ought not *he* to be taught compassion, who was to hoard the product of the earth, before dispensing it to starving nations? Might not a sudden elevation have fostered that spirit of pride, of which we see incipient traces in Joseph's early life? In telling his early dreams he predicted the future, in a manner so offensive, as not only to excite the angry passions of his brethren, but also to bring upon him a rebuke from his father.

But whatever his natural disposition may have been, it was necessary, that he should learn humility and compassion in the school of affliction. He who had been a bond-slave, learned humility. He who had been wrongly accused and imprisoned, learned the value of justice. He who had wept for himself, learned to weep for others. And so affliction did its appointed work, and it was withdrawn. The shepherd's boy became the mighty man. His shortlived affliction ended in unheard-of prosperity.

Thus, if we aspire after high place, if feelings of emulation are stirring within us, if we pray as well as labour for a position of eminence and usefulness among our fellow-men—laudable objects in those who are commencing life—remember, my brethren, you may be, at the same time, praying for much disciplinary suffering—it may be necessary for you to be involved in cares, from which less aspiring spirits may be exempt.

To these last-mentioned brethren, cares and sorrows may, nevertheless, be sent to arouse them from indolence and self-indulgence. This is however so obvious a case, that, as time presses, I shall pass on to observe, that although the Lord doth not willingly afflict the children of men, it may be necessary for Him, as the King Eternal, Invisible, to involve us in calamities, for the sake of others, as well as for a punishment to ourselves.

For this purpose I will remind you of the case of David.

We see David a man after God's own heart; full of faith, and, because full of faith, fearless in the midst of danger; surmounting all difficulties; trampling over his enemies; ascending the throne; a prosperous and a patriotic king; raising Israel from a tribe to a nation, taking the lead amidst all the nations around.

We see him a prophet. His spirit (as the Psalmist) seems to be in unison with the church in every age, under the gospel as under the law. To him we are indebted for the greater portion of our Liturgy. He, the sweet singer, performed those prodigies of valour which made him worthy to become himself the subject of song. We see him the worthy object of a grateful people's admiration, loyalty and love.

But David fell. The viceroy of Jehovah surrounded himself with the oriental magnificence, by which the monarchs around him were distinguished. Like the despots around him, he began to regard his will as law, and forgot the law of his God. Courtiers were ready to carry his commands into effect, however unjust they might be. His conscience was hardened; and his moral sense was paralysed.

Until rebuked by Nathan, he scarcely felt a pang of remorse for his deed of darkness, in the case of Uriah and his wife. He had only done, what the kings around him had done before him, and would do again.

But when the Lord spake by the mouth of His prophet; when the call to repentance came; the heart of David responded to the call, and the king was prostrate before his God,—a penitent. His heart regained its tenderness, and overflowed with grief. His repentance, how deep it was, may be seen from his penitential Psalms. He was overwhelmed by a lasting sense of guilt, shame, remorse. His cry for mercy was suppressed; he dared not speak; but the unuttered prayer was audible by Him to whom all hearts are open. David was pardoned. The Searcher of hearts knew that his repentance was sincere. No penance was required. No conditions were prescribed. No services demanded. The Blood of the Atonement had a retrospective efficacy. The sin was blotted out. The words are few, but they are striking words. "David said unto Nathan, I have sinned against the Lord. And Nathan said unto David, The Lord hath put away thy sin." David thought only of his God. He recked not of the consequences. He had loved his God. He had offended his God. This love returned. He sorrowed for having offended the God whom he loved. And how vast the consolation of knowing that when repentance is sincere,—a sorrow flowing from love to God—it is, at once, accepted through the merits of Jesus Christ our Lord,—the Lamb slain from the foundation of the world.

And now David rose up a pardoned sinner. Though sorrowful he could still rejoice. He resumed his duties as a King, as a Prophet, as the Psalmist.

We are all of us, at best, but pardoned sinners. And some among us know, from experience, the joy past utterance, that is felt, when, after a season of repentance, a voice is heard within us, speaking to the soul, and saying, "Go and sin no more."

But David's sin had reference to others besides himself. David had given occasion to the enemies of God to blaspheme. To the present hour the blasphemy is heard;—the sarcasm of the sinner, who is proud of being accounted a sinner, so long as his sin is not what the world calls dishonourable: he laughs, with the ungodly laughter, which is intended to make infidel the weak-hearted, and points to the man who was once a man after God's own heart.

All this was foreknown, and on this account the same prophet, who was commissioned to say unto David, "The Lord hath put away thy sin," was directed to foretell the temporal afflictions which, from that day, made David's life on earth a life of woe.

From the time of his fall to the hour of his death, the sword did not depart from David's house. His child was taken from him, notwithstanding his prayer and fasting. His daughter was dishonoured. His family was disgraced. His favourite son rose up in rebellion against him. Counsellors, who had learned wisdom, sitting at David's feet, conspired against him. The once triumphant David was obliged to fly from his ungrateful capital. In his humiliation he was reviled as a bloody man. He was insulted by Joab. He was not permitted to accomplish the work which he had contemplated, as that which was to be the glory of his reign. The Temple was erected by his son.

Not a murmur; not a word of complaint escaped the lips of the pardoned penitent; not a syllable of deprecation. He, in his penitence, thought only of the Lord, "Against thee only have I done this evil." He looked upon all that he now suffered, as but the chastisement of a father who scourgeth every son whom he receiveth. He traced it all to God. The feeling, which supported him in his trials, is sufficiently indicated by what he said, when Shimei cursed him, and said, "Go up, thou bloody man, thou man of Belial." "So let him curse," said the penitent, the humiliated king, "because the Lord said unto him, Curse David. Who shall therefore say, Wherefore hast thou done so?"[1]

The Lord had pardoned him. This sufficed; and amidst all his afflictions, he had that peace within, which passeth all understanding, and is a foretaste of that sweet rest awaiting the servants of the Lord, —there, "where the wicked cease from troubling, and the weary are at rest."

Let those, however, who are yielding to temptations in any of the various forms, in which it assails the young, lay this history to heart; and remember, that

[1] 2 Sam. xvi. 7, 10.

although repentance, when sincere, is always accepted, —from the consequences of their sin in this life there is no promise that they shall escape.

It were easy to multiply examples of that principle upon which God is pleased to act when He sees it to be necessary to afflict the children of men.

But only to one more case shall I refer; and I refer to the history of Job, since the revelations in that history were intended to enable us to understand, why it was necessary, that our blessed Lord and Saviour Jesus Christ should be emphatically The Man of Sorrows.

Job is a type of our blessed Lord; and in his history we see that, while a righteous man is under the protection of God, his virtues may be tested and made perfect by temptation and sorrow.

When we say, then, that the Lord Jesus Christ came to obey, we imply that He came to suffer. How could we know that He could in all things bend the human to the Divine will, unless He were tempted? And what is temptation but a sorrow? We know, from the book of Job, the logic of Satan. The servant of God is tried in small things,—and he resists temptation, obeying God. If he does not fall, as our first parents, on the first temptation, a more painful temptation must be permitted; and then, on his resisting that; a temptation more painful still,—until the trial is brought to that point of suffering that human nature can bear no more, and in his death the martyr triumphs.

The infidel accuses the Christian of supposing, that God found pleasure in the sufferings of the only sinless human being that ever trod this earth. The Christian's answer has been already given. Even in that miracle of mercy, by which the Incarnate God effected the salvation of man, God could not interfere with the constituted order of things. It was to sustain that constituted order of things, (the laws of nature in the moral as well as in the physical world, and extending to angels and all the hosts of heaven, as well as unto man,) that the Lord from heaven came: and submitting to that order of things, He proved the sinlessness of His life, by rendering obedience to God, under trials such as none but the God-man could have sustained.

His trials began with His birth. He was born to poverty. Conscious of possessing powers, which might have shaken the world, and have raised Him to the pinnacle of human greatness, He not only did not exercise those powers to rescue Himself from the troubles attendant upon His condition of life, but He resisted, for thirty years, the greater temptation, to relieve, by an exertion of His miraculous powers, the wants of others, or to instruct their minds. They who have felt in themselves the generous impulses, which hurry the young into action, will regard our Lord's unrepining submission to a life of obscurity, (until His call came), as one of the great miracles of His life; while at the same time it evinces His entire obedience, the submission of His man's will to the will of His Father which is in heaven.

I need not dwell upon those trials which proved the perfection of His obedience, when His ministry commenced, and when He, the Lord of all, was despised and rejected of men.

We will only remind you how, as the end drew near, His heart was lacerated,—His very soul was agonized;—how in all the dearest relations of life He was wounded. Like one wave upon another, affliction after affliction came down upon Him; but still in all things He was obedient. When human nature could bear no more, It was finished; His sufferings—man's redemption. He obeyed even unto death, and it was finished. Heaven was re-opened to our race,—and yet more than this, heaven was now brought down to the very heart of man, and regenerate man has become a temple of the Holy Ghost.

When our Lord was in His agony, an angel was

sent to comfort Him. Superhuman comfort He required, in order that He might bear that pressure of affliction, which caused Him to shed, as it were, great drops of blood,—and superhuman aid was granted, when He stood alone in the world, forsaken by those He died to save; but *His* comforter was not the Holy Ghost, for the Holy Ghost was not yet given.

One with the Father and the Son, the Holy Ghost as God is eternal,—He never had a beginning, for He is from everlasting; but it was not, until the work of the Redeemer was finished upon the Cross, that He condescended to assume an office in the Church,—and to come, as He now cometh into the hearts of the regenerate, a more than Comforter,—the Paraclete.

Oh blessed be the name of the Lord Jesus Christ! He sendeth the Holy Ghost to be the consoler of His people. He strengthens their faith, He enlarges their hope, He brightens their charity; and in this strengthening of faith, this brightening of hope, this enlargement of charity, He causes them to feel that the kingdom of heaven is righteousness and peace and joy in the Holy Ghost.

And so we conclude. The object of this discourse has been, not to discuss, as in an essay, the deep things of God, which are better adapted for study in the closet than for exhortation from the pulpit; but simply to impress upon the mind of the hearer the consolatory results of Christian faith. Christianity, when realised to the soul, imparts a happiness, which the world can neither give nor take away, or even understand. If we turn in earnest unto the Lord, and if our hearts are sanctified by grace, we shall find, in very deed, that godliness hath the promise of the life which now is, as well as of that which is to come: it is happiness in hand as well as heaven in reversion.

SERMON X.

GOD THE REWARD OF THE FAITHFUL.

BY

THE REV. W. J. BUTLER, M.A.

VICAR OF WANTAGE.

SERMON X.

PSALM XVI. 12.

Thou shalt shew me the path of life; in Thy presence is the fulness of joy: and at Thy right hand there is pleasure for evermore.

IN the truly "golden" Psalm, which these words conclude, the writer, certainly "the sweet Psalmist" himself "of Israel, the man who was raised up on high, the anointed of the God of Jacob," dwells and enlarges upon the blessedness of that perfect communion with the great and living God which had sustained him already, and which was about to sustain him, to the very end, in the many changing scenes, in the difficulties, sorrows, and great anxieties of his eventful life. Being, at the time of writing it, according to reasonable conjecture, an outcast[1]; driven

[1] V. Thrupp's *Introduction to the Psalms*, Ps. xvi.

from Jerusalem by the jealousy of the moody Saul; taunted by the king for his very poverty and helplessness in the words, "Hear now, ye Benjamites; will the son of Jesse give every one of you fields and vineyards, that all of you have conspired against me;" his friends, the priests of Nob, cruelly murdered for innocently supplying his need;—he casts himself upon a more solid and certain stay than he can find here on earth, and having, it may be, in mind God's promise to that tribe to whom no inheritance or land is given, "for I, said the Lord" to Levi, "am thy part and thine inheritance," he too—of the tribe of Judah—yet a Levite in heart and spirit—self dedicated and accepted—boldly claims the same. He looks to that guidance, which has led him onwards from his youth up even till now, and exclaims, "The Lord is the portion of mine inheritance and of my cup: Thou maintainest my lot." He recognises the wondrous dealings of God with him, the marvellous elevating and refining process which has been at work within him since the days when, as a simple shepherd, he kept his father's sheep on the mountains of Bethlehem; and, tried as he is by cruel persecutions and suspicions, by false friends and open foes, with no prospect before him except long years of suffering, he nevertheless hesitates not to assert that "the lot is fallen unto him in a fair ground, yea, that he has a goodly heritage." And what is that heritage? What is left to him, beggared, oppressed, and desolate, save One and One only, even the Lord Himself? *This* is his possession—his true possession—his abiding possession—which, under no circumstances whatever, can possibly fail him. "I have set God always before me; for He is on my right hand, therefore I shall not be moved." Of this not even the grave can deprive him. There too, it still is his. "My flesh also shall rest in hope. For Thou wilt not leave my soul to hell, neither shalt Thou suffer Thine holy one to see destruction." It is his own even through eternity. "Thou shalt shew me the path of life; in Thy presence is the fulness of joy; and at Thy right hand there is pleasure for evermore."

What, my brethren, are such words as these but true songs of triumph? What earthly success, what earthly glory or possessions could ever draw forth the like from man's lips or heart? Do we not feel, as we hear them, that we have in them the utterances of a conqueror, nay, of more than a conqueror; even of one who is kept in "perfect peace," and that "because his soul is stayed on God"? And have we not here vividly brought before us, as in some bright picture, the whole subject of our meditation this night, namely, how completely and amply to all who will accept and refuse not His love, GOD Himself is indeed the REWARD of HIS OWN, that is, of HIS FAITHFUL PEOPLE? May God, in His mercy, enable us to lay hold of this great and blessed Truth, and lead us to perceive that there is indeed within our grasp—if only we will "feel after it and find" it—a Gift so precious—a Blessing so great—a Reward so glorious—that to gain it and make it ours, we might well, like St Paul, "suffer the loss of all things, and count them but dung!"

And that we may realise this—that we may see the wondrous blessedness of this mighty Gift of God Himself, given by Himself to us—let us investigate one simple question—Wherein, especially, does true happiness consist?

Is it not, above all, in that which, in the highest sense of the word, we may call Rest? By this I mean, not the dull unintelligent rest of sleep, or mere inactivity, but that sensation which accompanies freedom from care and anxiety, from uneasy longings which can never be gratified, from possibility of disappointment, from the uneasy sense of loss and waste, from bitter boding of retributive pain closely dogging the heels of present pleasure. This is no inactive, useless state. So far from it, is it not then above all—when the man is thus at Rest—that he has really the best chance of developing all that is in him, and bringing all his talents to perfection? As on the imperturbed calmness of night, the growth of all things seems to depend; so the man, unruffled by agitating passions and wearing anxieties, can then best expand his nature and fulfil the object of his being.

But observe, this Rest, this power of being at Rest, belongs, of all the functions of man's being, to the heart[1] alone; or, in other words, to the seat of his affections. The body, for instance, is not that which rests. It is not made for Rest. On the contrary, manifestly in this world it is made for change. Change is its natural condition. It is never in one stay. It moves continually. It is ever growing, dwindling, decaying, passing away. Necessarily, it is fed, indulged, gratified over and over again, and still it craves. Nor can the mind, if we understand by this the intellectual faculty, find Rest. Is it intended that it should rest? To press ever onwards, aiming ever at more than it has as yet attained—at higher, deeper, knowledge; to make one truth mastered but the stepping-stone to other truths; struggling on,

[1] V. Newman's *Parochial Sermons*, Vol. v. p. 357.

weary and yet not satiated; like the mountain traveller, who pants onwards towards some inaccessible, and ever retreating summit; is it not thus with the ever active, ever restless, mind of man?

But the heart *can* rest. And why? For this reason, because love satisfies the heart, and the heart can love; yea, is such that it can love Him who, being Himself infinite, is—if only He gives Himself to be loved—at once and for ever all that love can crave. And then, if the heart by thus loving Him, be at Rest, it will follow that, notwithstanding all the turmoil and stir of life, of our fretful bodies, and busy, active minds, the whole man will be at Rest and peace. Like some monarch the fountain of honour, the heart sits in her dignity, dispensing Rest, and with Rest, happiness and joy to the whole being of the man. As the heart is, so is all. And the Rest of the heart consists in its being filled with that love for God, with that perfect certainty of His love given in return, for which, in its wondrous capacity for love, He manifestly contrived and formed it. It needs little to prove this. Take, for instance, any of those interests which men strive to put in the place of God—praise, earthly honour, power, pleasure, self. Will these indeed satisfy? Or does not all experience prove that they are far too meän and puny for the dignity of the heart of man? The insatiate conqueror, craving still for fresh conquests, stands weeping at the ocean. The great emperor, arrived at the very summit of his power, ruler of half the civilised world, arbiter of the fate of Europe, in mid life flings away his crown, and buries himself in the solitudes of St Just. What tragedy was ever more piteous than that book of accomplished wishes and broken hopes and unsatisfied affections, which the philosophy of our own generation so loves to quote? He, the Solomon, great king of earthly peace, has gained all that earth can offer. He has had his fill of all things—mirth and pleasure, wine, wisdom; great works, such as only Eastern despots can accomplish; "vineyards, gardens, pools of water." He recounts his vast possessions—"cattle great and small, gold and silver, peculiar treasure of kings, men and women singers—all delights." He lacks not the highest intellectual cultivation, the deepest human knowledge, the most perfect worldly wisdom. He is eminently and in all things successful. "I withheld not my heart from any joy; for my heart rejoiced in all my labour:" "and this," he adds, "this joy was the portion of all my labour." But all will not suffice to bring him Rest. Still is his heart empty, its affections unsupplied. After all, what is he but a fool? In all this there is not one ray of real love to cheer him. He has discarded love, and love has in turn left him. For

> 'He that shuts out love, in turn shall be
> Shut out from love, and on her threshold lie
> Howling in outer darkness.'

And so on the great king's mind, the aweful truth fails not to burst. "I looked on all the works that my hands had wrought and the labour that I had laboured to do: and, behold, all was vanity and vexation of spirit, and there was no profit under the sun."

Or even where love is, if it be earthly love, however pure and noble, still the heart cannot rest. Take it in its very noblest form—in that which, from its purity, unselfishness, and devotion, approaches most nearly to heavenly love—the friendship and attachment of two kindred spirits. Even this, sweet and comforting, cheering as it is, and elevating, will not suffice. Even here fickleness and doubt, and jealousy, can enter in and mar. Nay, in the very nature of things, the intimacy of friendship can scarcely last for more than a short time, seldom indeed through life. As life passes on, the old friendship dwindles and wanes, lighting up, it may be, on certain special occasions, but in the end slowly yielding to separation, difference of interest, and occupation, till the intimate loving friends of youth are scarcely any longer aware of the existence of each other—and, as the eye carelessly glances over the record of death in some daily journal, it lights upon the name of one with whom in days gone by deepest thoughts have been interchanged, or the victory won in the glowing contests of youthful strength—or the hours of study brightened by union of labour—or the day of rest solaced by long country-walks—and with a short sigh the old friend, for a single moment, recalls the past, then passes on his way, and thinks of it all no more. Nay, even that which God has appointed as the special earthly comfort of man—the love of woman in its most perfect form—in the wedded life; even this lasts only, in the touching words of the marriage-vow, "till death us do part;" and broken and desolate, as we often see, is that soul, in the hour of separation, which has rested upon this alone.

Thus then by that sense of utter blankness which the heart experiences when it loves not, by the absolute incapacity of all earthly things to fill it, by its own strong cravings and yearnings, we learn that it is His will that its real and best affections should be concentrated on Him alone. Even as the needle rests from its strange uneasy trembling, then only when it points true to the pole, so the heart can then only be at Rest, when it is filled with the love of God.

And therefore He who made the heart such as it is, most freely and willingly gives Himself to our love. As to Abraham, in the days of old, when He called him from family, home, position, wealth, sending him landless and friendless into a distant and unknown land, so to each one of us, as he forces us to feel that these things are not sufficient for the energies and affections of the heart, does He, who ever "giveth liberally"—offer even Himself. "I," He says, "I Myself," the great Almighty Triune God, "I am thy Shield and thy exceeding great Reward."

But possibly, my brethren, putting the matter in a practical form, you ask, is not this after all a mere figure of speech? How can I *realise* this? I understand the meaning of earthly satisfactions. I can enter fully into the blessedness of having earthly friends. I can commune with them. I can use treasure or lands. I perfectly appreciate the meaning of such as these. But in what intelligible sense can it be said that God is my reward? How does He act upon me? How can I *enjoy* One so infinitely above me, or feel other in the thought of Him than constraint and weariness and fear?

Believe me, hard as it may seem, the joy in the love of God is practical enough, even as it is within reach of all. To gain it, I freely grant, an effort is needed. And, doubtless, in order to realise God as to be able to love Him, the heart needs to be educated and trained. If indeed God, who alone *can* satisfy our hearts and give us rest, *is* to fill them, we must learn first of all to set aside our own fancies and speculations and to view Him even as He is, that is, as He makes Himself known to us. And I hesitate not to say that even as He alone can meet the demands of love, so only He Himself, *as He has revealed Himself* to us, *can* be truly loved. I must think of Him, for instance, as in the truest, highest sense, a distinct and real Person. I cannot love an Idea. An Idea may be admirable, interesting, absorbing, graceful. I may be struck with its truth, its power, its symmetry, its ingenuity. A neighbouring nation boasts that it goes to war for it. But I cannot love it. It will not answer to my heart's requirements. If God is but an idea, formed within and dwelling within the precincts of the human mind, I cannot find in Him that which will satisfy my soul in its deep cravings, not for finite but for infinite love. Neither again can I love a subtile Essence spread throughout the universe, a sort of general soul, underlying all things, a diffused Deity, having no separate existence, everything at once and nothing. Neither can I love a Deity, of which I myself am an integral portion; and my own voice, or the general voice of man, the exponent. Such definitions, or more properly speaking, such tamperings with the Being and Glory of the great God of Heaven must necessarily shut out the very possibility of love. Miserable comforters are they all! Woe, woe to him who would feed that hungering, longing soul of his on such paltry husks as these, who hews out to himself these broken cisterns, holding no water!

Is it not the fact that these unworthy imaginings, this fear to *own* God as He really is, this clinging to human explanations—these bubbles blown off by human pride and vanity—lie at the root of half man's misery, and half man's sin? Look, if you will, at that self-satisfied young cynic—in his pride of fancied intellect—with lip contemptuously curling at the very sight of all those who cling to the old faith and the old path and the old teaching and the God of their fathers. Search deeply within his heart. Mark, in spite of the "Who's afraid?" external attitude, his real doubt of himself, and of his miserable scepticism.

Does he never feel a single qualm of anxiety, nor tremble when the excitement of society and the desire of applause are for the moment lulled? What has he gained in exchange for a definite Faith and a true living God on Whom to concentrate his faculty of love? *Truth*, he will perhaps proudly—though not without a dash of affectation—answer. Yes; but is he sure that he has found the truth? Or is he not rather beating upon a stormy sea without compass or stars to guide him? He has lost—Faith, Love, Hope, the anchorage of the soul to Heaven. His whole being is in a state of spiritual ferment. And too probably, at least in lower natures, as all experience goes to prove, Epicureanism, in all its frightful and unsatisfying carnality, will at the end take possession of him, and mould him for its own.

No, my brethren, the *heart*, the best guide in spiritual things, assures me of it, in order that I may love, that my affections may be rightly expanded, I must dwell on the thought of God as He reveals Himself to us—that is, as a Being distinctly separate from all—in His Threefold Personality of Father, Son, and Holy Ghost. I must strive to image Him to myself as Truthful, Merciful, Almighty, Eternal, One who is Himself full of Love, Wisdom, Justice; Who knows all things, guides all things, not as leaving them to the action of some broad, general, fate or law, laid down once for all, which binds even Himself, like an Æschylean Zeus, but superintending all things, "upholding them by the word of His power," nicely adjusting them for their own well-being and for His own glory, in which lies indeed the happiness of all. Such an one, beyond and external to me, yet in me and near me, "dwelling in that light to which none can approach," yet "about my path and about my bed," watching over me and caring for me, ready in the hour of need to help me, dealing with me even as a father with a beloved son, such an One I can love. The thought of Him is enough to fill my heart. I can feel that I have indeed something when I am assured that I possess His love. When I think of it, I can exclaim, in the words of the Psalmist, "I will love Thee, O Lord, my strength. The Lord is my stony Rock and my Defence, my Saviour, my God, and my Might, in Whom I will trust, my Buckler, the Horn also of my salvation, and my Refuge." I can find in Him all that is needed to draw forth my love. I can speak to Him, I can obey Him, I can look to Him, reverence Him, adore Him, love Him "with all my heart, and with all my mind, and with all my soul, and with all my strength."

And is it not for this special purpose, namely, that He may thus be ours, and, as it were, within our reach; that we may appreciate the blessedness of possessing Him; in a word, that we may be able to love Him; is it not for this that He vouchsafes to humble Himself to man's level, and make the Revelation of Himself to man in all the imperfection of human language and of human thought? Do I, for instance, read that God was wroth, that He repented, that He was grieved? Do I find continual mention in His revealed Word of the Eye, the Ear, the Hand, the Voice, the Arm, the Back Parts, the Face, the Mind of God —that is, of Him Who is without parts or passions, the great Almighty Spirit, Who "hath not flesh and bones," Who "is not a man that He should lie, or the Son of Man that He should repent"—of whom the Apostle asks, "who hath known the Mind of God, or who hath been His Counsellor?" And how am I to understand all this but as the merciful guiding of my Heavenly Father, leading me to look to Him as One Whom the heart can in a measure realise, whose Personality can, however faintly, be presented to my intellect? I believe in Him as One who, by the effort of His Divine Will, performs those acts which He gives to man to perform by the various organs of their being. I read of Him as being the Judge of all the earth, and therefore I know that He is not a mere function of earthly things. I know that if He rewards and punishes, He cannot be a mere soul of the Creation. If He acts and speaks, He can be no Idea, but a real and living Person. And therefore I can fix my thoughts and my heart upon Him; believe that, as I commune with Him, He will hear me, and, in His wisdom, answer. And therefore He is such that I can love.

But again. Is there not a higher teaching even than this, a more distinct giving of Himself on the part of GOD to the Love of the human soul? He would not only assure us of His love, revealing to us His mighty Name, and, so to say, in the abstract, those attributes which draw forth the love of man, but lest the heart, unskilled in spiritual things, should still hold back and hesitate, in order that the very human portion of our affections may be satisfied, our love of human friendship, our craving for lips speaking to lips, and hand grasping hand; that we may learn to appreciate even with our bodily senses the Sweetness, the Loveableness, the Perfection of Him whom it is permitted to us to love—therefore is God Himself "made flesh and dwelt among us." As "the Man Christ Jesus" He vouchsafes to speak to man, drawing us, in the words of the Prophet, "with the cords of a man." Hungering, thirsting, weary, seeking human sympathy, moving that pity which is "akin to love," He, being God, stands before us in the very flesh of a deeply loving Man. He chooses for His own solace human friendship. He calls His Disciples "Friends." He asks for their love. "Simon, son of Jonas," He asks His chief Apostle, "lovest thou Me?" Their love, as how could it fail to be, is kindled towards Him. "Let us," cries one, "go, that we may die with Him." We cannot contemplate Him without seeing in Him One altogether to be loved, The "Chiefest among ten thousand," in Whose love the heart can altogether repose, in peace and joy and rest.

This then is the reward of God's faithful people. This loving God, all Wise, all Tender, all Sympathising, all Great, all Sufficing, revealing Himself as Man to man, is He who gives Himself to the human heart to satisfy its longing for love. He who made the heart such that it yearns after Him, and can find no peace but in Him, Himself becomes its portion. "They shall be my people, and I will be their God." "I will dwell in them, and walk in them." "I will never fail them, nor forsake them." "Behold, I stand at the door, and watch. If any man hear my voice, and open the door, I will enter in, and sup with him, and he with me."

See I pray you how all this really affects and touches us. Meditate, if you will, however slightly, on the life of man. Think of it in all its strange uncertainty—its disappointments, dangers, sorrows. Think of the aweful suddenness with which grief and misfortune fall, in overpowering and overflowing floods, crushing and sweeping our hopes and our joys before them. And then weigh the utter inability of man, left to himself and his own feeble resources, to make head against them. See, for instance, that loving united well-nurtured family dwelling in the midst of blessings,—opulence, ease, respect; the very darling of a neighbourhood, enjoying, as such households enjoy them, the choicest gifts of earth. All has ever gone well with them. They have never known real sorrow; they look forward to nothing but more honour, greater wealth, still more perfected and intense enjoyment. This is no exaggerated picture of the condition of thousands of our well to do English households, in this land of wealth and peace. Then lo! like lightning the long delayed grief darts into the very bosom of that happy graceful circle. Most commonly it comes in the form of that which no wealth, no earthly prosperity can hinder, the message of disease and death. The son, in the very beginning of a career of promise, is struck down. The daughter, but a twelvemonth since, quitting the parental roof in all the triumph of young wedded life, lies, a mother indeed, but with life fast ebbing forth, which no human skill can stay. Or on the father, or the mother, the prop and pillar of the whole, the irresistible hand has lighted in fearful and hopeless suddenness. Or take another case. Long and eagerly, nay more, devotedly, has the man toiled through life. Earthly rest, such as it is, is at length within his grasp. He has at length earned the long looked for competence, goods laid up for many a year. He will retire and enjoy himself; his future dwelling selected and purchased, his own, smiles pleasantly upon him. He furnishes it, gathers his friends around him, talks cheerfully of this or that improvement. Then scarcely has he settled down, when the pang of pain in some vital part, faintly it may be felt before, but now sharp and piercing, awakens him to the knowledge that his time is nearly come, his hours numbered, that in truth nothing really remains to him but to make ready for the grave. Such cases as these are common everywhere. We all recognise in them what has again and again happened under our eyes. It seems almost needless to dwell upon them. And yet unless we do so, we cannot rightly estimate the value of that wondrous Reward which God's Presence brings to the soul wherein he vouchsafes to dwell. "Thou shalt shew me the path of life." Is it not indeed something in all this weariness and sorrow, amid these tears and pains and doubt and uncertainty, this disappointment and utter ruin of our hopes, to be sure at least of One, to know that we have One who can be and who is ever the same, "without variableness or shadow of turning"—ever constant, true, loving, all-sufficient, "who, in the midst of the troubles which we have in our hearts, sends His "comforts" to "refresh our souls"?

Nor need we wait for sorrow to feel the blessedness of this Presence—this mighty gift of God Himself to the soul. Is it not indeed true, that, just as our whole nature is most developed by the close companionship of some great and true friend, so in the highest degree this will be to the soul, which is ever conversing with God, which ever owns and realises His Presence, and, like Enoch, "walks with" Him. Are not in Him all "treasures of wisdom and knowledge," all that trains the intellect as well as fills the heart? Will not the mind continually brought into contact with Him be marvellously purified, and strengthened? Will not that Presence ever acting upon the man bring him on to the full perfection of his nature, harmonising to him all the discords of life; yea, giving a meaning, which nothing else can give, to our intricate and complex being, and filling the soul for ever with cheerfulness and joy? "Thou, O God, hast taught me from my youth up until now, forsake me not in mine old age, when I am gray-headed, until I have shewed Thy strength to this generation, and Thy power to all them that are yet for to come." "This God is our God for ever and ever, He shall be our guide unto Death."

Yes, my brethren, as in life, so in Death—in Death the great trial of all. If God be indeed in life the reward of His people, is He not, if we may say so, tenfold more in Death? In Life we may after a fashion dispense with God, putting Him altogether from our mind and heart. It is possible to immerse ourselves in pleasures, business, society, even though they satisfy not. But how is it *then*, when by the sorrow of those who love us, by the tears which *will* fall, by our own inward consciousness, we feel of a truth that our time has at length come, that there is no more comfort, or even interest to be gathered from earthly things, that Eternity in all its terrible boundlessness is opening before us, that our trial, our judgment, our eternal doom is now close at hand. How can I bear it—how pass through it—on whom can I rest or stay? Then above all does the heart learn what it is to have the great God of heaven its own, its friend; to be upborne in those His everlasting arms; in His mighty strength to tread down the lion beneath the feet. Resting calmly on that gracious Presence then vouchsafed, the reward of long service and love, the faithful soul can look boldly through that dark passage, and even from the midst of mortal agony, while the yells of the savage multitude are ringing round him—with the wild beast, the fire, the cross, in full presence before him—can nevertheless exclaim, "I know Whom I have believed, and am persuaded that He is able to keep that which is committed to Him," that soul which has given its faith and love to Him "until that day." The philosopher may indeed bleed calmly to death, rehearsing his lines of pathetic poetry, but all the enchantments of philosophy or science cannot simulate the Christian's real joy and peace, nor teach the heart to exclaim, "Though I go through the valley of the shadow of death, I will fear no evil: for Thou art with me: Thy rod and Thy staff comfort me:" or "I am ready to be offered; the time of my departure is at hand. I have fought a good fight; I have finished my course; I have kept the faith. Henceforth there is laid up for me a crown of righteousness which the Lord, the righteous Judge, will give me at that day."

Lastly, if God be the reward of His people in life and in death, what is He in Eternity? "At Thy right hand there is pleasure for evermore." What is all Life but the preparation for this? What is all His love expended on us in this present time, but the preparing of the heart to receive Him fully and entirely; to "behold the King in His true beauty, in the Land which is afar off"? If even here He has filled our hearts with joy and thankfulness, what shall it be there where no jarring of the fleshly nature, no earth-born clouds of human passion, can ever enter to obscure His Presence from the soul, or shut out the perfection of His Glory? Then shall He give Himself freely and unreservedly to His people's gaze and love. "They shall drink out of His pleasures as out of a river." All their faculties, perfected and glorified, shall find full play. They shall be "like Him:" wise in His Wisdom, holy in His Purity, strong in His Might, glorious in His Brightness, undecaying in His Eternity. God Himself, that is in some wondrous visible Presence, shall dwell among them, and be their God. "They are before the throne of God, and serve Him day and night in His temple and He that sitteth on the throne shall dwell among them. They shall hunger no more, neither thirst any more; neither shall the sun light on them, nor any heat. For the Lamb, which is in the midst of the throne, shall feed them, and shall lead them, unto living fountains of water; and God shall wipe away all tears from their eyes.

What then remains, my brethren, but that now, even now, we claim our Christian privilege, and use our glorious Gift, and open our hearts freely that the Reward of God's Presence may be ours? Sitting on His throne on high, the great God of Heaven invites us to make Him our own; offers us the strength of His mighty Presence in Life, in Death, in Eternity. Hereafter this shall be ours, without pain or effort. For the present we must make it our own by a distinct effort of Faith. *We* must seek Him, to be however amply rewarded, even in this time. Shall we not then make that effort? Is it not our wisdom boldly to search for Him, ask for Him, jealously maintain all that is His—His word, His revealed Attributes, the great truths of His Incarnation? What more blessed than to bring ourselves continually into direct communion with Him, our souls in Prayer, in Service, in Sacrament, under the very light of His Countenance; offering ourselves daily to Him, Body, Soul, and Spirit; crying to Him again and again in loving confidence, "Whom have I in heaven but Thee, and there is none upon earth that I desire in comparison of Thee? My flesh and my heart faileth; but Thou art the strength of my life, and my portion for ever."

SERMON XI.

MOSES WITH GOD IN MOUNT PISGAH.

BY

THE VERY REVEREND

HARVEY GOODWIN, D.D.

DEAN OF ELY.

SERMON XI.

DEUTERONOMY XXXIV. part of ver. 6.

No man knoweth of his sepulchre unto this day.

ACCORDING to our modern views of the burial of great men,—indeed according to the views which have prevailed at all times amongst civilized nations,—this brief record of the sepulchre of Moses is very striking. Most of us remember the imposing character of the ceremony with which we committed to the ground, some years ago, the remains of the greatest Englishman of modern times, the great Duke of Wellington. No event in our own days has called together a larger number of people; every one was desirous of witnessing the funeral of the man to whom this country and the whole of Europe were so deeply indebted: it was regarded as a high privilege to know and to see his sepulchre. And though the contrast between the pageant of a funeral and the active work of a living man is sufficiently obvious, and though some may be tempted to sneer at the homage paid to the mighty dead and to say that so grand a ceremonial is out of place, still the general sense of mankind is in favour of such homage, and approves of imposing ceremonies connected with the sepulchres of the great and good. It seems as though we should do violence to our own feelings, if we should make small account of the resting-place of the dead; the graves of the departed teach good lessons to the living; and it is doubtless with the belief that it is for the benefit of the nation to hold (as it were) a communion with the spirits of its great men and its benefactors, that we sanction public funerals, and bury some of our most distinguished men in buildings like S. Paul's Cathedral and Westminster Abbey.

But the desire of shewing respect to the dead, as we call it, the desire of consecrating and honouring the tombs of those whom we honour and love, is no modern thing. One of the most touching stories in the book of Genesis is that which tells us of Abraham buying a plot of land, in which to bury Sarah. Abraham was then a stranger in the land which God had promised him, and which his seed were to inherit; and when Sarah died, we read that Abraham wept for her, and then "he stood up from before his dead, and spake unto the sons of Heth, saying, I am a stranger and a sojourner with you: give me a possession of a burying-place." Finally, a bargain was made, and "the field of Ephron and the cave which was therein, and all the trees that were in the field, were made sure unto Abraham for a possession;" and this burying-place not only became the property of Abraham, but was his only property, the only abiding pledge of his interest in the land of Canaan, as landlord by divine right, until his seed came out of Egypt and conquered the country.

Thus, in the earliest history of God's chosen people, we find a reverence for sepulchres; and so in like manner, when the people came to be settled in the land which God promised them, we read of "sepulchres of kings," and of the notable men being buried "with their fathers." There was no superstition in this; superstition no doubt has been connected with sepulchres and the remains of the departed, but this was a form of idolatry into which the Israelites do not seem to have fallen; no, it was the natural outcoming of human feeling; it was the manifestation of a desire to be not wholly separated from the departed, it was something like a foreshadowing of the Christian doctrine of the "Communion of Saints." And the feeling found its highest opportunity of exhibiting itself, when it became connected with that sepulchre, round which we shall gather in imagination on Good Friday: *that* is the Sepulchre of sepulchres; emphatically, "The *Holy* Sepulchre," the sepulchre which sanctifies all others and from which they derive their dignity. Every one *knows* of the Sepulchre (so to speak) of Jesus Christ; it is one of the world's "holy places;" there they laid His sacred body, there it was watched by a guard, while the stone which closed the sepulchre was sealed; and if it be in any sense true, that "no man knoweth of the sepulchre" of Jesus Christ "until this day," it is only true because He is risen from the dead, and His sepulchre has ceased to be a sepulchre for Him, who is ascended up into heaven.

Now I say that with all this reverence for sepulchres, shewing itself both in ancient and in modern days, the statement in the text concerning the burial of Moses must appear very striking. Looking upon it from the divine side, we can easily understand that it was better for the children of Israel that they should *not* know the burial-place of their great lawgiver, lest perchance they should be tempted to honour his dead bones and his sepulchre, more than they ought. Looking upon the matter from another point of view, we may perhaps say that if Moses and his doings had been as legendary and uncertain as some would make them, it is probable that a more ordinary and more gorgeous picture would have been given of his death and his funeral. Looking upon the history as the simple record of one who performed a most important part in the developement of the divine purposes, of one who, according to any conceivable scale of human excellence, must ever stand out as one of the greatest and best and noblest and wisest among the children of men, we may perhaps say that Moses being dead speaks to us even by his death, and that our ignorance of his sepulchre may teach us some important lessons concerning the grave, and, through the grave, concerning the eternal life beyond it.

Let us then for a few moments, Christian brethren, accompany Moses (as it were) in his ascent of Pisgah, where it pleased God that he should die. I will say nothing at present concerning the sin, in consequence of which Moses was forbidden to enter the promised land: sin is always more or less connected with death, and yet we can contemplate the departure of good men almost without a remembrance of the fact that death has a sting, and that that sting is sin: and therefore in the case of Moses, I will put out of sight for the present that rebellious act of his which shut him out from the promised land, and regard him only as a servant of God who has done his work, and who is going to his rest. "Moses was an hundred and twenty years old when he died; his eye was not dim, nor his natural force abated:" and yet he had done a good life's work: forty years of education in the wisdom of the Egyptians, forty years of training in the rougher school of the desert, and then forty years of hard and toilsome and thankless work as leader of a rebellious and stiffnecked people. If the value of a man's life is to be estimated by the amount of comfort which he finds in it,—worldly comfort, I mean,—then I fancy that few lives would be less satisfactory than that of Moses: his early days might have been comfortable enough, though even then I should suppose that the suffering condition of his people must have embittered most of the sweets which he enjoyed in Pharaoh's palace: but those early days over, there was little of peace and comfort remaining: it was all laborious work, and work against the grain. Moses was a modest and retiring man; it was through no forwardness of his own that he became ambassador to Pharaoh; his post was one of difficulty and anxiety; and from the moment that he undertook his mission to the end of his life all ease was gone. Even when he had got free from Pharaoh, his difficulties and anxieties were only beginning: he might have found comfort and satisfaction, if the people had been grateful and gentle and obedient; but they were all that is opposite to these qualities, and the burden of their sins seemed to fall upon Moses; he was their lawgiver, their leader, their prophet, their intercessor, —everything. A hard and painful post doubtless; but Moses did his work in the fear of God, and at length his evening of rest came. God summons him to go up into Mount Pisgah, thence to see the promised land, and there to die: and Moses makes all due preparation to obey the summons, he puts his house in order, he gives his last exhortations and warnings to the people, he hands over his charge to another, and then with unabated strength and apparently without sadness, he climbs the mountain which God has appointed.

According to human estimate it must have been a weary climb: to leave the society of men and of friends below and go up into a mountain, with the knowledge that there is to be no return, is enough to try the nerve and the spirit of the boldest and strongest. Every man no doubt must die alone, but for good men the loneliness is much softened by the presence of kind friends and the solemn ordinances of religion: and the picture of the patriarch Jacob (for instance), with his sons and his sons' sons round his bed, is very different from and much more cheerful than the picture of Moses going up from his family and kindred and friends to die alone upon Nebo. And yet after all we feel that the death of Moses was not a melancholy event; and if we ask the reason it is not far to seek, and the reason is this, that God was with him in the mountain; God was with him in his loneliness; God was with him in his death. We read that "the Lord shewed him" from "the top of Pisgah" the promised land, now lying within reach (as it were) of the people whom he had brought out of Egypt, and "the Lord said unto him, This is the land which I sware unto Abraham, unto Isaac, and unto Jacob." It was not the mere seeing of the land which was sufficient to comfort the heart of Moses; it might even have had the opposite effect; it might have made him feel sad and disappointed and unhappy to find himself so near to the land of which he had often told the Israelites, and then to be compelled to give over the command to another, and to lose the glory of leading his people into their promised home. But then it was the Lord who shewed him the land; God was with him, and he knew that God was with him; and therefore he knew also that all was well, that there were good reasons why he should not lead the people over Jordan, that there were good reasons why Joshua should. In fact, if God's promises were only fulfilled, if the people really inherited the land, what matter who led them in? Was it not enough that Moses had been employed hitherto? and when a man, whether in a high place like Moses, or in a simple humble place like many of us, has done the work which God has appointed him to do, why should he not be content and say, "*Nunc dimittis*—Lord, now lettest Thou Thy servant depart in peace"?

Yes, it would be an injustice to the character of Moses to suppose that even a single thought of sadness or disappointment crossed his mind, when God shewed him the promised land. Of all the saints of ancient time there is perhaps not one who exhibits so fully the self-sacrificing spirit, which it is the glory of the Gospel to have rendered more abundant than it was in olden days, and of which we see the perfection in the character of our Lord Jesus Christ. Ever for the people, never for himself; even when the choice was put before him of the destruction of the whole nation and the making of himself a nation greater and mightier, his eyes were not dazzled by the prospect, but he still pleaded with God for the rebellious children of Israel.

And it is the reward and blessedness of this heavenly type of mind, that all things seem to come right, and that self-sacrificing men are strangers to ten thousand griefs and disappointments which self-seekers have to bear as best they can. So it was that the death of Moses was free from sadness; and I note that it seems to have been unclouded by the only circumstance which could well have thrown a gloom over it. The sentence that he should not go over Jordan was in the first instance a punishment. Moses had been rash, had not glorified God before the people on one memorable occasion: and without examining into the precise nature of his sin, it is sufficient to say that its punishment was the not being permitted to go into the promised land: this was the dark remembrance in Moses' history, and we might perhaps have supposed that in the view of Canaan from Pisgah this remembrance would have become painfully bright. Sometimes past sins *do* thus rise up in after days, and cause great pain and sorrow: and especially if a man be alone with God, as Moses was, we might expect that a sin closely bound up with the circumstances of his death would be painfully called to mind. Hence I notice particularly, that the history is altogether silent concerning the fault which excluded Moses from Canaan: "I have caused thee," said the Lord to Moses, "to see the land with thine eyes; but thou shalt not go over thither"—the prohibition, you perceive, enforced, but the reason of the prohibition (as it were) forgotten: it is as though God in His mercy would refrain from wounding the heart of His faithful servant; He has forgotten Moses' offense; He has cast it into the deep of the sea; and now He will shew Moses the bright land of promise, and cheer his heart with the thought that his work has not been in vain, and make him glad with the knowledge that God's promises will be fulfilled, and that the people of the promise will inherit the land.

So Moses died; and God was with him in his death. God taught him that he was still a sojourner and a stranger; but He pointed his eyes to a land now not very far off, a type of that land of promise which in this life is brought nearest to us, when we are brought nearest to death. And when Moses had used his eyes, which were still undimmed by age, to contemplate that happy land, then God closed his eyes, and then God buried him. And if no man was permitted to know the place of his sepulchre, we must observe that this also is true of those two men whose departure from this world has been the most notable, the most glorious; no man knows of the sepulchre of Enoch; no man knows of the sepulchre of Elijah; and even of those who have chiefly glorified God by their deaths, the Apostles and Martyrs of the Church, there are many of whom it may be said, that of their sepulchres also we know little or nothing. But in truth, Christian brethren, what matters it concerning a man's sepulchre either to himself or to the world? The question is, not what will become of our poor bones when they have ceased to be the ministers of a living soul, but what becomes of our lives while they can be made useful in the work of God, and of our bodies while they can be presented to God as a living sacrifice and as the instruments of a reasonable service. Yet this it is well to bear in mind, that whether our sepulchre be a lowly one or the contrary, still a sepulchre each one of us must have, and the work of life is to prepare for that sepulchre and for the life which lies beyond it. Do we want an example of the way in which we should prepare? then, I would say, that no better example can be found than that of Moses in the mountain with God. What had been *his* preparation for that last solemn meeting? It was the doing of God's will during a long laborious active lifetime. No life could be more completely given to God than that of Moses. If any man might adopt without irreverence the words of our Lord, "I came not to do my own will, but the will of Him that sent me," certainly Moses might adopt them: apparently making no provision for his own wants, and no preparation for his own meeting with God, but ever labouring to supply the wants of the people and to guard them against meeting God unprepared. And in thus ministering to others, he ministered to himself; in taking care of other men's souls, his own was not neglected; working for God strengthened his own spiritual life; and the discipline which he had undergone, in the busy and anxious life that he had spent as leader and lawgiver of a rebellious people, had made him meet for the inheritance which God had prepared for him. Here, I think, is a good lesson for us, and comfort for hard-working busy people. Is a man working for God in the station in which God has placed him? is he endeavouring to minister to the wants of his brethren, as opportunities permit? is he fighting God's battle against evil? Then he may be sure that God's Holy Spirit will work with his spirit, and cause his labours to bring back a blessing upon himself. I do not mean of course that any man can make himself meet for the inheritance of the saints; but I mean that an orderly, courageous, honest, earnest effort to serve God in our stations, and to benefit others, and to preach the gospel to the poor, will be the best and safest way of ensuring both in life and in death the blessed presence of God.

This is the way also to guard against that horrible evil, which I can hardly pass by without mention, the evil of having to do a work of repentance when God calls us to Him to die. The activity of Moses in life, his cheerfulness in the Mount with God, may well suggest to us how important and necessary it is that all spiritual work should be done, before that night comes upon us in which no man can work. The time of our departure from this world should be, like that of Moses, a time of quiet communion with God: there should be no outstanding accounts (so to speak) of sins unrepented: at the very best there must always be a deep sense of unworthiness, but there should be no new lesson to learn, no work to begin, no discovery to make concerning the character of God and the deep sinfulness of sin.

And if we do make this good use of the day which God has given us, then perhaps we also, like Moses, may be called up from the world to meet God in the mountain, and from thence see the promised land before we die: our lot more blessed than his, inasmuch as we are not forbidden to enter the promised land. Death is usually spoken of as a valley, not as a mountain; David says, "When I pass through the valley of the shadow of death, I will fear no evil;" and certainly to go *down* to the grave seems the more natural notion, and a mountain does not appear to be a very appropriate symbol of death. But on this very account it is perhaps all the more noticeable that when Moses, the servant of God, was called upon to die, God summoned him to the top of Pisgah. The obvious reason was that he might be able from thence to see the land to which he had conducted the people; but if we may venture to put a spiritual meaning upon such a fact of history, we may perhaps say that there is something bright and cheering in the notion of God's servants being called *up* to Him to die. The picture brought before our eyes by the history of the death of Moses, is not that of an infirm old man sinking down into his grave, but that of an aged servant of God, having still all his powers and his faculties, mounting up above the level of the world to meet God, who is waiting for him. Certainly the summons, "Come up to Me to die," is the brightest and most cheering announcement possible of our departure from this world; and the Ascension of our blessed Lord from the Mountain into Heaven, following as it did His sorrowful going down into the tomb, seems to teach us that a going up to meet God, rather than a going down into the grave, is the true form of departure for the servants of the Lord Jesus Christ.

Lastly, let me remind you, Christian brethren, that, whether in life or in death, to rise above the level of this present world and to be alone with God is the best privilege of every Christian soul. It was not the first time that Moses had been alone with God in the Mount, when he went up to die; he had been, as you know, with God on Mount Sinai, when God gave him the Law. Nor indeed was it the last, for the three favoured disciples afterwards saw him in glory with the Redeemer Himself on the Mount of Transfiguration. But especially observe that it was not the *first* time, and that it was because Moses had been alone with God in life that he could without fear be alone with God in death. Ah! that being alone with God in death is easy enough, if we have climbed the mountain and sought His presence in the time of our health and strength. Therefore I would say, as a suitable termination to these Lenten Sermons, strive thus, dear Christian brethren, in the times of your health and strength to climb the mountain and to be with God. There is much to catch your fancy and please your appetites in the plain below; and the ascent of the mountain is somewhat steep, and the path rugged, and the necessary effort great:

nevertheless "tarry not in all the plain, escape to the mountain, lest you be consumed." God is calling you; God is helping you; Christ Himself went up the Mount of sorrow, that you might be able to follow Him. Even for the youngest and the strongest, there is no time to spare.

> Once gain the mountain top, and thou art free:
> Till then, who rest, presume; who turn to look, are lost.

CPSIA information can be obtained
at www.ICGtesting.com
Printed in the USA
LVHW040023180422
716440LV00005B/475

9 783752 594805